CRUEL CONSEQUENCES

A CONSEQUENCES NOVEL
BOOK 2

AMANDA SIEGRIST

McCord Family Novel

Protecting You

Trust in Love

Deserving You

Always Kind of Love

Finding You

Dare You to Love

Mona & Mason

The Paranormal Chronicles, Volume I

Perfect For You Novel

The Wrong Brother

The Right Time

The Easy Part

The Hard Choice

Psychic Love Novel

Exploding Love

Captured Love

Slaying Love Novel

Won't Let You Go

Doomed Love

Deadly Crazy

Evidence of Sin

Finding Redemption

Obsessed Hope

Short Stories

Paint By Murder

Follow Me, Sweet Darling

Sleighville Novel

Dashing Through the Fear

Here Comes Chaos

The Last Noel

Standalone Novel

The Danger with Love

Conquering Fear Novel

CO-WRITTEN WITH JANE BLYTHE

Drowning in You

Out of the Darkness

Closing In

Hello, dear reader!

You will notice in the first few chapters that I have writing prompts listed. I enjoy writing weekly flash fiction and you lovely readers give me prompts. This story started as flash fiction. Sometimes the best stories start that way. So sit back, relax, and dive into this intense, romantic suspense.

Happy reading and much love,
Amanda Siegrist

1

WRITING PROMPT ~ THE PERFECT
PRESENT. PINK AND YELLOW. WHO'S
THERE? MAKE YOURSELF KNOWN.

SHE SET the bouquet of dahlia flowers on the ground and
took a small step back.

Pink and yellow.

Such two vibrant, happy colors. Just like her sister.
Always so carefree and laughing and loving life. And her
sister loved dahlias, especially the pink and yellow ones.
The way the two colors merged with such finesse and
beauty.

The perfect present—for a birthday her sister wouldn't
be able to celebrate.

Briella's eyes zoned in on the headstone, her sister's
name etched in the granite forever.

Dawn Suzana Colton. October 14, 1992 - October 14, 2022.
Forever in our hearts. Beloved daughter and sister.

Silent tears slid down her cheeks. She couldn't tear her
eyes away, even when she ached to twirl around and leave.
Run far away and never come back. Leave the pain behind.

But she would never run. Never leave. Never stop until
the man who killed her sister was caught.

"Happy birthday, Dawn." Briella blew her sister a kiss and turned around.

She could only handle visiting her grave for so long. A few minutes, no more than that. She rarely spoke, only stared at the headstone. Some people came to feel closer to their lost loved ones. Some people liked to share good news or vent about life as if the person were still alive and could respond. Some people thought people who visited graves were odd.

Honestly, Briella wasn't sure what category she fell into. Now and again, she felt the need to visit and then leave.

Did she feel more at peace once she left? No.

She felt nothing but intense rage and hatred for the injustice surrounding her sister's case.

A year had passed and still no leads on who killed her sister. No evidence, no witnesses, no answer to why someone would break into her sister's apartment—on her birthday, no less—and rape and brutally murder her.

Anytime she closed her eyes, she could still see her sister's body sprawled on the bed, her clothes torn, her body bruised and slashed...blood everywhere.

Shaking off the memory, she increased the pep in her step. Perhaps this hadn't been the best idea to come visit her sister's grave on the anniversary of her death.

But...it was also her birthday. She deserved recognition for that. Especially since Briella never had the chance last year. She had arrived at her sister's apartment too late.

Her pace increased even more.

A little too much when she tripped on a patch of recently disturbed grass. Landing hard on her hands to brace her fall, she winced when a sharp pain raced up her right hand through her wrist and to her shoulder.

Rolling awkwardly from her knees to her butt, she

cradled her right arm as her eyes glided back toward her sister's grave.

Was it considered a bad omen to trip and fall in a grave-yard? Because as she stared hard at the loss of such sweet innocence, it felt like a bad omen.

The snap of a branch had her twisting her head to the left. More headstones, a few trees dotted here and there, but otherwise, nothing odd she could see.

A shiver rushed down her spine.

The same kind of terrifying shiver that had scorched her skin when she stepped inside her sister's apartment. Even before she had seen her mangled body.

"Knock it off, Briella. It's the day. It's...it's going to be a rough one."

Inhaling a deep breath, she then exhaled slowly, taking one more sweep of the area.

Still, nothing looked amiss.

Well, she refused to wallow in self-pity. She refused to let the grief consume her. She refused to let the nightmares take control where she would never be able to resurface.

That only left one option to regain her equilibrium. To take all her erratic emotions, her pain, and center it on one thing.

Detective Stromberg.

———

HE WAITED BEHIND A LARGE HEADSTONE, sensing her still looking around, yet he didn't dare take a peek. That had been a close call. She had almost seen him. Thank goodness for the large headstone nearby.

Of course, there had also been a tree close-by as well, which was how he had stepped on a small branch. It probably fell from the recent thunderstorm they had a few days ago.

But the headstone had been closer. So he immediately ducked low, scrunching his knees close to his chest, and waited.

He didn't find it odd sitting against a headstone or on top of someone's grave. Not much gave him pause. He felt comfortable in his skin and any kind of predicament he always found himself in. He was lucky in that regard because he knew not everyone was as confident in themselves as he was.

Why shouldn't he be confident?

He got away with murder.

Inhaling, he tried to detect Briella's scent. A sweet lavender aroma that always tickled his senses into delicious thoughts. On occasion, he liked to roam her apartment. She didn't wear perfume, not like some women who liked to douse themselves with a disgusting amount. No, her beautiful scent came from lotion. On one risky adventure into her domain, he had watched her lather herself from head to toe with the lilac scent. Of course, not wanting to give himself away before he let his urge take over, he left as quietly as he had appeared.

He was good at that. Coming and going without anyone noticing him. He was invisible.

Untouchable.

Although, he wasn't a fool. He never did unnecessary things. Like right now. He couldn't catch a whiff of her scent. His hands fisted, irritated at the fact. He couldn't get closer without her seeing him because then the jig would be up. If he was one thing, it was careful. Very, very careful in every decision.

They had yet to find out he killed Dawn Colton.

Of course, it hadn't been his intention that night. He had only wanted—

Best not to conjure old memories at a time when he needed to keep his senses tuned to his surroundings. He might've made a mistake that night, but when the bloodbath had ended, he'd done his due diligence to make sure not a trace of him was left behind.

Since they hadn't knocked on his door to arrest him, he knew they'd never find out that he'd killed her.

When Briella didn't call out, "Who's there? Make yourself known," or even a simple "Hello?" he knew she had dismissed the strange sound as nothing more than nature speaking its natural sound.

He heard soft footsteps drifting away as if she had finally decided to leave the area. Risking a glance, he peered around the headstone, watching as Briella walked with brisk steps back to her car.

He continued to wait patiently in his spot until she was in her car and it sped away out of his view.

Standing up, he wiped his pants both front and back from any grass or dirt that might've attracted to him and headed for his vehicle. Of course, he had parked farther away, nowhere near the cemetery. One could never be too careful.

It was how he always stayed one step ahead of the police —ahead of Detective Stromberg.

Ah, yes.

Detective Stromberg.

That would most likely be Briella's next destination. She didn't make it difficult to decipher her moves. She was very rigid in her routine.

Sleep, eat, work, repeat. Throw in a visit every two weeks

or so to Detective Stromberg, and that was it. She rarely deviated from her routine.

With today being a very special day—Dawn's birthday, and unfortunately the day she died—he knew Briella would pay Detective Stromberg a visit.

Which meant so would he. Away from prying eyes, of course.

He knew a shortcut. He'd make it there first.

He didn't want to miss the scene between the two. Their meetings were always volatile.

He loved it...

But only if Detective Stromberg didn't do something he didn't like.

"I HATE it when you drive. Can you drive any slower?" Tate muttered as he tapped his knee.

Stromberg shrugged and let his foot off the gas pedal a little more. "I'm not going that slow. What's the rush?"

He knew he wasn't in any kind of hurry to get back to the precinct. It was terrible of him, but he didn't want to see Briella. And he knew he'd see her today, considering it was the one-year anniversary of her sister's death.

A whole year had passed and nada. What kind of detective was he? Sure, no detective had a one-hundred percent case-closed rate. But this case...he should've solved it. Just to give Briella some peace.

He jerked when Tate slapped him on the shoulder. "What the hell, asshole?"

"I felt you slow down even more, jackass." Tate's level stare said he was ready to jump across the seat, push him out of the car, and take over.

Yeah, so maybe he had. He wasn't about to admit it though. Because that would bring questions forth, and Tate would insist he talk about it, and talking was the last thing he wanted to do.

"No, I didn't."

"You totally did."

"Whatever, I didn't."

Tate huffed. "Asshole."

He scoffed. "Jackass."

Then silence descended. A comfortable, normal silence that usually followed after one of their common arguments. They were still new to being partners, with Tate moving to New York only five months ago. They didn't get along when they first met, and everything that followed, well, it had brought them closer together.

But they still liked to call each other names. It was always said in an affectionate voice. Sort of. Anyone who didn't know them would assume they were being serious.

"I'm sorry."

Stromberg tossed a glance at Tate, then drew his gaze back to the road to take a right. "You running a fever? You okay? I just drive into the *Twilight Zone*?"

Tate chuckled, then sighed and relaxed in his seat. "No, you heard me right. I apologized."

Yeah, but the question was why? For some terrifying reason, Stromberg didn't want to ask.

"I know what day it is. I know why you've had us running around all morning and most of the afternoon following dumb leads for our latest case. I thought I could get through the day not saying anything, but I can't."

Just his luck.

Tate had to have a damn conscience. And be a damn good friend.

In a moment of error when he tossed Tate the wrong file, he learned all about The Raptor case and Briella. It was amazing Tate never met Briella; she stopped by the precinct often enough asking about her sister's case. But he was either out doing something on another case or in another part of the building. It's as if fate had decided Tate shouldn't meet her yet. Or at all. So talking about the case was the last thing he wanted to do.

Two months ago, when Tate found out, he had walked through the crime scene, went through each part of the case with a fine-tooth comb as he had and...nothing.

No evidence. No leads. No nada. Simply a brutal murder of a beautiful woman who didn't deserve to die so young.

"You can't ignore her."

His hands tightened on the wheel.

"You might not be willing to tell her how you feel, but you can't ignore her. Not today, man. It's not right."

It didn't matter how true Tate's words resonated with him. He couldn't see her today. Of all days.

What would he say?

Nothing comforting, that's for sure. A year had passed, and he had yet to make her feel an ounce better. He was an epic failure.

"Stromberg?"

"Stop...please, Tate." His jaw clenched, hoping nothing else slipped out. They might call each asshole and jackass and a slew of other offensives names, but he didn't want to *mean* it in this moment.

They headed to a few more stops, questioning an old friend and a neighbor of the latest victim in the murder case that had landed on their desk two days ago. It seemed like a pretty easy case. The boyfriend did it. They only needed to dot all the I's and cross all the T's before they arrested him.

But if one read between the lines, he was stalling. He was scared of one tiny woman who could send his heart into a crazy erratic mess with one glance his way.

They didn't make it back to the precinct until six o'clock.

He breathed a sigh of relief when he didn't see Briella sitting on the steps to the front door of the precinct. It wouldn't be the first time he'd caught her there.

Tate didn't say anything other than chuckle low under his breath.

He let out another sigh of relief when he didn't notice her sitting in the lobby waiting for him to arrive. When it was cold out, she sat in there sometimes as well.

When they walked into the large room where most of their desks were set up, he almost released his third sigh of relief. Until the chair in front of his desk swiveled around and the one woman who haunted his nightly dreams pinned him with a desolate stare.

All the air rushed out of his lungs.

Wow.

He *was* an asshole. No doubt about it. He'd been cruel staying away from the precinct all day knowing she'd show up. Instead of getting this inevitable meeting out of the way, he tried his hardest to avoid her.

The sad, melancholy expression in her amber-colored eyes had him feeling like the lowest cad on earth.

Tate wasn't one to mind his own business, so he did what he always did when they returned. He sat down at his desk. But he had the decency to not make eye contact with her and started to input their latest interviews into the computer.

"Where've you been?" Briella moved the chair back and forth as if she were getting ready to do a full three-hundred-sixty-degree twirl.

His brows puckered low as he processed how to respond. His typical response would be to throw back a condescending retort. Because that's what they did. They fought like two lions trying to mark the territory as theirs. Even when he didn't *want* to act that way with her. She brought it out of him so easily. He also sensed she didn't want to be coddled by anyone, least of all him. So he dished it right back.

"Honestly, avoiding you." Then he averted his gaze to the floor, shocked he even uttered that. He should've gone with his typical arrogant response instead.

His chair made the short squeaky sound it always made when he stood up.

He never considered himself a coward, and he wouldn't start now. He met her gaze when she invaded his personal space, getting so close, he was tempted to close the distance and kiss her. Wipe away her painful memories and fill her day with something other than death and despair. But that would put him in the disrespectful and disgusting category. He wasn't *that* much of an asshole. Only a semi-one.

"I'm hard on you, I know." She nodded as if she needed to agree with herself. Water gathered in her eyes. "I know you've been doing your best. I want answers."

God, he ached for those same answers. He wanted to give her the peace she so desperately prayed for.

"One of these days, I will give you those answers. I promise."

Her gorgeous amber eyes bore into his as if she could see to his very soul. "Are you supposed to make such promises? You've never done that before."

His hand ached to reach up and brush her black hair behind her ear, then make a quick sweep across her lips with a tender kiss.

Shake it loose. You can't cross the line, no matter how much you want to.

Even the three little words he said all the time to Tate simply to annoy him didn't stop the impulse. His hand lifted and caressed her cheek before drifting back down by his side. Her eyes widened at the contact. Yeah, he didn't know why he did it either. Shocked the hell out of him too.

He leaned closer so no one else—not even Tate—could hear him.

"For you, Briella, I would do anything to see you smile, to take the pain away, to erase the torment in your beautiful eyes. I shouldn't promise anything. But you have my word, I will solve your sister's case."

She shook her head as if grappling for the right words, then to his shock, she stepped around him and walked away without one word.

And he had to cross the line even more. What a fool!

So much for telling her how he felt, something Tate told him he should do. Not that he necessarily told her how he felt, but she could infer and read between the lines what he actually said.

He liked her.

Hell, the way he constantly thought about her, dreamt about her, worried about how she was doing—he loved her.

He gave his word, and he never went back on his word.

Which meant he *had* to solve her sister's murder.

Or face the consequences.

The very brutal consequences of breaking Briella's heart.

2

WRITING PROMPT ~ SHE SURPRISED
HIM WITH HER ATHLETIC SLAP.

BRI SLAMMED her apartment door shut. Her purse made a loud thud when it hit the coffee table in the living room. She didn't even care that some of the contents slipped out. Her main goal was the bottle that sat on the kitchen counter.

Whiskey, straight. She liked a small glass every night. It soothed her rattled nerves and helped her sleep. She never drank more than that because she never wanted to become something she would regret.

Their mother had been an alcoholic. From the earliest memories of her childhood, she remembered the drinking. The slurred words as her mother attempted to read them a bedtime story. Then their father having to pull her mother out of the room and finish tucking them in. Then the ensuing fight they could hear through the walls. She figured her father had tried to be quiet as he berated her mother for, yet again, drinking. But her mother was never a quiet drunk.

She didn't even want to think about the times the police would show up because the neighbors called about the loud noises. Usually her mother throwing things—and all the shouting matches.

Dawn never drank. She didn't even try alcohol—not once. Bri couldn't help herself. She wanted to know why her mother loved it so much. Her first sip had been a beer her friend had nabbed from her parents' stash in the garage. Gah! It was disgusting. From there, she tried little sips of other drinks until she found the one she didn't mind on occasion.

Whiskey. Strong, yet sizzling as it slid down her throat. A burst of warmth and then a numbing sensation.

Wine she could tolerate on occasion as well.

Before Dawn's death, she rarely imbibed. Now, she had at least one drink before bed. Every single day. And because some nights were so bad—the nightmares, the memories— she damn near emptied the whole bottle until everything went numb. Her mind, her limbs, even the memories.

The glass she pulled from the cupboard shook in her hand as she stared at the whiskey bottle. The cap hadn't even been cracked yet. A brand new bottle sat waiting for her to demolish. Oh, God, if she opened it, she'd drink it all. She knew herself that well.

Her gaze glided to the clock near the fridge.

6:43 PM.

In roughly another two hours, it'd be an exact year from when she found her sister's body.

The glass clattered to the counter, rolling until it stopped just short of the edge. Bracing her hands against the cream-colored countertop, she squeezed until she could feel pain in her palms. She held back an anguished scream. If she screamed, one of her neighbors would call the cops and she didn't want to deal with any cops. She'd had issues with her neighbor below her. The last thing she needed—tonight of all nights—was her neighbor tattling on her again for loud noises.

Of course, if the cops were called...

One cop could show up.

She bowed her head as she replayed the odd scene that occurred at the precinct.

The tenderness in his eyes. The understanding, as if he honestly knew the pain she was suffering. The desire...

It hadn't been obvious until he softly, just barely, grazed her cheek. And then his sweet, honest words that shattered her heart and the thick wall she had erected around it, especially from him.

She didn't know when she started to develop feelings for him. But it happened. Most of the time, she shoved it down, ignoring it as best as she could. She found herself visiting the precinct, demanding answers, but also relishing the fact she could see his handsome, adoring face. Hear his sultry voice. Their encounters were usually volatile, with her being the loudest—thanks to her mother. She would have a glass —or two—of whiskey before seeing him sometimes. He'd never commented that he could smell the alcohol on her breath or see her actions were off-kilter, so she never knew if he suspected anything. What could he do anyway? It wasn't against the law to drink or confront a detective about her sister's murder after having a few glasses.

At first, her thunderous outbursts started because she wanted answers. Then it turned into a defense mechanism. Something she couldn't stop. She couldn't allow him to get close, to get under her skin, to seep into her heart.

It was wrong.

Her sister was dead, and she didn't deserve happiness when her sister didn't even have the choice anymore.

It was her fault she died. If only she would've—

Her hand swiped the glass and slammed it hard to the counter as her other hand went for the bottle.

Her entire body shook as she grappled with herself.

To drink or not to drink.

She couldn't take it!

She slammed the glass again—even harder against the counter.

This time it shattered.

The decision whether to drink or not was snatched away from her as she stared at the large piece of glass sticking out of the side of her hand.

Oddly enough, she didn't feel much pain. But these days, she rarely felt anything but despair and desolation...except when she was near Detective Stromberg.

Blood trickled out.

"Oh, shit, oh, shit, oh, shit, Bri," she muttered as she pulled her hand closer, yet she didn't remove the piece of glass. She was afraid if she pulled it out, the bleeding would gush like a geyser.

Calmly, although with shaky steps, she walked to the coffee table and grabbed her phone that had shuffled out of her purse when she tossed it.

Her dominant hand—thankfully not the one injured—trembled as she dialed 9-1-1. Not one of her best moments. Not that every officer knew her, but most, at least in Detective Stromberg's precinct, did.

An officer she didn't recognize was the first to arrive, followed by a paramedic, who took one look at her hand and his eyes widened. She knew then she'd be making a trip to the hospital for stitches. He complimented her on her good thinking of not removing the piece of glass. Not only because it was so deep, but because if not removed properly, she could've inadvertently pulled out some part of the glass and broken other tiny chunks off without even knowing, which could've caused an infection.

Once at the hospital, everything turned into a blur. She didn't feel any pain as they removed the shard from her hand. It helped that they used an anesthetic agent to dull everything.

Or it might've been the fact she turned her mind off, ventured to her happy place to block out the commotion. She did that on occasion, simply shut her mind off.

Sometimes, she had even done it at work, which her boss was not particularly fond of. The jackass hadn't even given his condolences when her sister was murdered.

"What the hell, Briella?"

She jerked at the sound of the harsh tone, jarred out of her wandering thoughts. Her gaze melted into Detective Stromberg's baby-blue eyes that held a mixture of anger and worry.

He inhaled, swiped a hand down his face, then the anger that had been prominently displayed disappeared. Only worry and concern filtered into every facet of his expression.

No.

No, that wasn't right.

She didn't want his worry or his concern. She didn't want him to say nice, caring things to her. She didn't want him to do anything but what he normally did: tell her he was doing the best he could and he'd update her when he had any new information. That's all she wanted.

Looking away from him, she glanced at her hand that was wrapped with white gauze. When did that happen? A sharp, throbbing pain hit her system, making her wince.

"Are you okay? Do you need anything? Should I go find the nurse?"

Oh, she hated the distress in his voice, as if he was truly distraught. Could she use some pain medication? Hell, yes. Was she about to admit it? Absolutely not.

She obviously missed everything. From the moment they pulled the glass out, to flushing out the wound to making sure no particles of glass stuck around. To stopping the bleeding, to stitching the side of her hand, to wrapping it with the gauze. Even the doctor had left the room. She zoned out all of it.

To be back in her happy la-la land where nothing bad could touch her. Oh, to have that bottle of whiskey sitting in her lap so she could drink straight from the bottle. Screw using a glass. No need to repeat the mistake pulsating through her hand.

Or not. That damn bottle was why she was sitting in a hospital bed with an annoyingly attractive detective two feet away from her.

She felt him move closer, yet she didn't look up.

"It's very strange you're not saying anything. You usually can't stop speaking when you're in front of me. At least holler at me to leave."

Her bottom lip trembled. She bit it to stop the tears that threatened to flow.

"There's not a lot in my life that scares me. But when I heard a call went through to your address and an ambulance was dispatched, well, that scared the shit out of me. Today of all days."

Her head whipped up, her gaze seeking his.

His eyes, a pale blue, looked glossy as if he were holding back his own tears.

"It was an accident," she whispered, aching for his touch. Anything from him. Even a brush of his fingers down her cheek.

He ruined everything between them when he touched her so tenderly. Now she wanted to feel more. So much more from him.

He stepped closer. His thigh touched the bed as he laid his hand near her, yet didn't touch.

Life could be so cruel. Why would he initiate tenderness at the precinct and now hold himself back? What game was he playing? Touch her already!

"I'm sorry I tried to avoid you today. I didn't know what to say to you. It hurts me every time I don't have any new answers. I hate disappointing you. Today, I didn't want to have to disappoint you." His gaze lowered to her hand. "I still did, anyway. I'm an asshole, and I'm sorry."

"And I'm a cranky bitch. I'm sorry I'm always so hard on you. I don't mean—" Her voice broke as the first tear escaped, followed by many more.

As if he finally heard her silent prayer, his arms wrapped around her as the tears poured out of her like a gushing waterfall.

STROMBERG SHUT THE DOOR QUIETLY, although he was tempted to slam it. The silence grated on his nerves.

For a few brief minutes, she was in his arms. Sure, she had been bawling her eyes out, and he hated hearing her pain. But she had been in his arms.

He wanted more of that—only without the tears.

And those thoughts had to stop in their tracks!

It didn't matter what Tate had said. That he should go for it and ask her out. *Screw the consequences* were his exact words. Getting entangled with any person involved in one of his cases was wrong. Not to mention against the rules. Talk about walking a fine line. A morally fine line at that.

Briella stopped in the living room and swiveled toward

him. "You didn't have to bring me home. You didn't have to escort me to my apartment. You can go now."

Well, yeah, he could.

He just didn't want to.

Not today.

She might not admit it, but today was not the day to be alone.

"You haven't told me how you hurt your hand yet. Care to tell me now?" He decided avoiding her demand would be better than arguing about the fact he wasn't leaving. Not yet, if at all for the night. It wouldn't be as a man wanting more; it would be as a detective being concerned. Yes. That was how he'd phrase it if anyone asked. Not that he'd allow anyone to ask him. No one needed to know he planned to spend the night. Watch over her and keep her safe—even from herself.

Hell, he wasn't sure *he* wanted to be alone tonight. He saw her sister's body like Briella had. Except, he saw it for a much longer period of time. He had to work the crime scene. Inspect her body, the area around it. He couldn't get her mangled body out of his memories. He couldn't get any of his cases out of his brain. They were all imprinted forever, even after he caught his perp.

Maybe that's why he named some of the killers with a ridiculous nickname. To make them appear not as horrific as they actually were. He couldn't say why or when he'd started doing it. It annoyed the hell out of Tate. He'd named Dawn's killer The Raptor as the slashes across her body reminded him of the dinosaur, a velociraptor. A predator. A killing machine. Dinosaurs didn't exist anymore and that made them less real. So, attaching that kind of connotation to the case made the horror less real. At least for tiny pockets of time. Plus, now that he knew Tate hated it when he dubbed killers with a nickname, he got perverse enjoyment out of it. He loved annoying Tate in any way possible.

She shook her head, her brows low, her lips tight. It was as if she were fighting an internal war with herself. To answer or not to answer.

He'd wait all night. He had nowhere else to be.

"I want you to leave." Her voice cracked and she didn't make eye contact, which told him she really *didn't* want him to leave.

"No, you don't." Then he grinned because maybe it would jumpstart her out of this...this...whatever mood she was in.

Briella was always in his face with a non-stop onslaught of words. Right now, she refused to meet his gaze, stood way too far away, and each word had a slight tremble in it.

"You don't know me. Don't pretend you do," she shot back, finally looking at him. But only for a moment.

He glanced around her small apartment—the living room and dining room connected—as he replied, "You're right, I don't know you that well. I'd like to change that."

Why did he say that? He shouldn't say things like that. He was the detective on a murder investigation, and she was the sister of the victim. There was so much wrong in that scenario for him to want more.

Her gaze slowly trailed to his. But she didn't respond.

He waited a few more seconds, hoping she'd say something—anything—to his bold words.

So much for Tate and his advice. *Yeah, tell her how you feel, that'll work.* Not.

"How about I get you something to drink? Like warm milk or tea or soda? Or whip up something to eat? Have you eaten yet?"

His only answer was a wide-eyed stare from her. She

looked confused and scared, like a small bird that had fallen out of its nest looking for its momma.

"Okay, I'll do that. Sounds like a plan."

If she wasn't going to respond, he'd pretend she had. This was why he couldn't leave her. She wasn't fighting back at all as he continued to take control of the situation.

Walking into the kitchen, he found his answer to how she cut her hand. Pieces of glass littered around the counter and on the floor with blood mingled in. Glancing around, he saw a few blood drops trail his way.

So she cut herself here and then made her way to the living room, which was where the trail led.

Picking up the large pieces of glass first, he then wiped the blood from the floor with a wet rag. After that task, he found a broom from the small pantry and wiped up the tiny particles of glass. Grabbing a new dishcloth, he wiped the counter as well.

He eyed the unopened bottle of whiskey and decided to tuck it away in a cupboard. The last thing Briella needed to do was get drunk. It wouldn't erase the pain of losing her sister.

Reaching for the bottle, a sharp voice stopped him before he made contact. "Don't you dare touch that."

Gazing at her a few feet away, he cocked a brow. "What are you going to do if I do?"

"Try it and see," she retorted with a bit of her normal flare she used with him.

Yes. Finally.

"You don't need to drink tonight. This won't solve anything. We'll—"

"There's no *we* here. Get out."

His eyes narrowed. "No."

Then he grabbed the bottle.

She surprised him with her athletic slap.

It came out of nowhere. She moved so fast and whipped her hand to his cheek, he had no idea it was coming.

His cheek stung, tiny pinpricks pulsating across his jaw. He let go of the bottle.

Her eyes rounded as she slapped a hand to her mouth. "Oh my God. I didn't mean to do that."

Then she fled the kitchen.

He heard only two sounds.

Tears once more.

And a door slamming.

3

Bri curled into herself, wrapping her body as tightly together as she could, shielding her face from his view. As soon as she heard her door creak open—the damn noise she could never fix or get the landlord to look at—she knew Detective Stromberg hadn't listened to her. He was still here. Invading her space.

Invading her heart.

Intruding in her bedroom of all places!

The bed dipped and the heat from his body as he sat close to her almost had her breaking her cocoon of safety to wrap herself in his arms instead.

"I'm sorry—again."

She inhaled sharply, then more tears ran down her cheeks at his whispered words.

He was sorry?

She *slapped* him. He didn't have anything to be sorry for.

But, of course, he was nothing but a gentleman. Even in all her tirades, her countless visits where she badgered him for answers, he never got downright cruel with her. Sure, he raised his voice and countered as good as she gave, but never with any malice behind his words.

She was sorry. And so embarrassed she hit him.

Oh no!

He could arrest her.

That horrible thought almost had her sitting up and begging for his forgiveness, but she didn't. Her defense mechanism was in full force. She tucked her arms tighter around her head and pretended he wasn't sitting so close to her. That he wasn't overrunning her senses and all the walls she carefully built against him.

"Briella..."

The soft way he said her name, like a caress against her skin, had her emotions soaring to a territory she always tried to avoid with him. Why did he have to whisper her name like a dying man looking for redemption?

She trembled when his hand landed on her shoulder. A touch so light, she wanted to cry out for more. Then it ventured down in a smooth stroke, yet still light as a feather, as if tempting her to follow the devil into the pits of hell.

His hand stopped short of her waist, a tiny shiver reverberating from his hand to her body.

Or maybe he was barely touching her because he was unsure of himself, of whether he should even be touching her.

He definitely shouldn't.

It only made her want what she could never have.

Then his hand disappeared altogether.

Another tear slipped away, sprinkling down her cheek in regret.

Regret for the love that could be but never would.

Regret because she had to push him away, to keep him at arm's length.

He had all but confessed he liked her minutes ago in her living room. She should be jumping for joy, not slapping him and shunning his affections and his thoughtfulness to keep her company on a day she didn't want to be alone.

But she couldn't. Her sister wasn't here, and she didn't deserve an ounce of happiness.

"Even though I should, I'm not leaving you. You can hit and scream and do everything you feel you need to do to me, but I won't leave. Not tonight." His short inhale had her anticipating another sweet touch from him.

But nothing came.

She wanted to scream and demand he leave once again, but like the coward she was, she stayed tucked away in her cocoon as if he couldn't touch her. Even in her mind.

Except, his insistence to stay by her side no matter what was igniting her desire for him so strongly deep inside, more tears wanted to escape. Tears of joy. Tears of happiness. Tears of relief that someone could still love her after what she had done.

Because if not for her and her foolish actions, her sister would still be alive today.

With that disastrous thought, her silent tears turned into heavy sobs, the only sound to fill the room.

Her entire body shook, yet stayed coiled like a snake hurting its prey.

His warm hand hit her shoulder once again, this time more firmly. A touch so strong, it was as if he were marking her as his. Instead of taking the same light path he had done the first time, he smoothed it over a bit and then ran it down her back. Down, then back up.

Comforting her.

Letting her know she wasn't alone.

Giving her the understanding everything would be okay.

All from one simple touch from his warm, steady hand as it ran up and down her back with the confidence that he had the right to.

Oh, how she wished he did.

Her sobs increased.

His hand disappeared.

She was disappointed and relieved at once. If she hadn't been crying so hard already, she would've started crying even harder until her chest and head throbbed uncontrollably from all the pain.

To her amazement, she was jostled out of her spot and landed in his lap. Her head rested comfortably on his chest as her body stayed curled into its position, but this time she wasn't able to shield her face. He could see all the tears streaming down her cheeks.

Then his hand resumed its path down her back in soothing strokes.

He didn't say a word.

She didn't protest.

If anything, her body tried to scoot closer, as if she could seep right under his skin and become one. Make him take her pain away.

The tears didn't stop. The shaking increased, her body so exhausted from releasing all her pain.

She had no idea how long she cried in his arms.

All she knew was she never wanted the moment to end. Because if she stopped and her tears slipped away, so would he.

And that proved how selfish of a person she truly was.

It explained why her sister died.

Because Briella only thought of herself, no matter what.

STROMBERG BLINKED a few times and started to stretch his stiff, sore body but stopped when it occurred to him *why* he felt so stiff and sore.

Briella was still in his arms.

Sunlight poured through the sheer white curtain covering the small window to his right.

She had cried deep, wrenching sobs that tore his heart apart that he couldn't do more to help the pain she was enduring. She cried until it turned into silence. Because he had been afraid to say the wrong thing, he said nothing. Eventually, she fell asleep. So had he, if the sunlight was any indication.

Which would account for every ache and pain his body was experiencing at the moment. He sat upright, although he had stretched his legs out in a comfortable position. Briella was still curled into his arms, her head resting on his chest. His arms were locked around her so even if she wanted to slip away, she wouldn't be able to without prying his hands apart.

He didn't regret a moment of it. And he knew he should. He should regret showing up to the hospital. Insisting he bring her home. Not listening when she told him to get out. Not even when she slapped him and proceeded to ignore everything he said to her in her bedroom.

He didn't want to be anywhere else.

He'd crossed that line and then some. As long as no one at work found out, it didn't matter. He'd keep doing what he was doing. Even then...he didn't think he'd change his behavior one bit.

A glance at the clock on her nightstand said he was late for work. Half past eight.

Shit.

He always arrived at work by seven, just like Tate.

He felt his phone in his pocket. He hadn't felt it vibrate from a text or phone call, which he would've, indicating Tate never called him.

Odd.

Tate was a lot like him. Maybe that's why they got along so well. Both were creatures of habit, did everything by the book—most of the time—and were never ever late.

He had called Tate last night letting him know he was heading to the hospital. Maybe Tate knew why he was late. Tate had even suggested he declare his feelings so she couldn't misinterpret anything.

He sort of did.

Or he hadn't heard his phone ring or vibrate because he'd slept great for the first time in a long time.

Nope. The regret still hadn't hit him.

But it didn't mean Briella returned his feelings.

She slapped him.

Well, okay. She slapped him because he reached for the alcohol—which they would be talking about whether she liked it or not. Although he couldn't begin to know the reasons why she slapped him, it didn't matter. He didn't hold it against her. Her emotions had been haywire last night. How couldn't they be. It had been the one-year anniversary of her sister's death. It would be hard every single year until he caught her killer. Even then, she would still live with the loss, the pain losing her sister had created.

But it would hurt less if she had closure. Some peace and knowledge of who—and even why—killed her sister.

As much as he wanted to remain here with her snuggled against his chest, he needed to get to work.

Bending slightly, he inhaled the subtle scent of lavender and then, because he couldn't resist, he pressed his lips to the top of her head.

She shifted.

He tensed.

It was one thing to kiss her. It was an entirely different thing for her to realize he had.

When she didn't say anything or keep moving or lift her head, he relaxed and thought about kissing her one more time. Even as innocent a kiss as it was.

But he decided not to press his luck.

He gently rubbed her arm, inhaled her alluring scent one more time, and then whispered her name.

"Briella, baby, it's time to wake up." The endearment slid off his tongue as if he had every right to say it. Getting slapped again wasn't high on his list. Especially right before he had to report to work. He had a beard, but it didn't mean his cheek wouldn't be red from the onslaught.

He felt the moment she became aware of her surroundings. Her entire body tensed. He couldn't be sure if it was because she was still in his arms or because he'd added the endearment. Probably both.

"Good morning."

He decided he'd try to skip all the awkwardness and pretend the entire situation was completely normal. Like it was any other day where she fell asleep in his arms and stayed there all night long.

She wiggled, which created the wrong reaction in him. Of course, the right reaction if the moment wasn't already awkward. But definitely the wrong time for his cock to announce it was ready to plunge deep inside her.

She stiffened once again.

He was at a loss for words. Sure, he dated. But only casual relationships where it never went further than a few months. Most women couldn't handle dating a cop. Especially one like him who worked long days and crazy hours.

He loved his job. Unfortunately—for the women—he always put his job first. He could be blunt and too honest at times. Not every woman appreciated that. And romance, well, that wasn't his forte either.

Maybe if he found the right woman...

"I don't know your work schedule. Obviously." He rolled his eyes. *You're an idiot. Shake it loose.* "But it's past eight and..." And he didn't know how to finish that sentence because he was a moron. Why should he care about work right now? For once in his life, he needed to put someone else first. Not his job.

Yet, Briella needed him to be focused on his job so he could find her sister's killer. Therefore, he should go. Right away. Not to mention if his captain asked why he was late today, he'd have to lie. Telling him he spent the night at her house, someone connected to one of his cases, would not go over well. He'd get a reaming and a firm reminder why it was a bad idea.

So he had to move his ass and avoid that kind of situation. He didn't want to lie to his captain.

She moved again, inciting his cock into further excitement. He inhaled sharply, refusing to acknowledge what she did to him. But damn... he was also dying to cup her chin and kiss her until every stitch of clothing between them disappeared.

Slowly, her golden eyes turned up to gaze into his. They were a myriad of emotions. Confusion, sadness... desire.

Then her hand reached up and smoothed across his scruffy jaw. Very, very bristled jaw. Some women didn't like he wore a beard, claiming it hurt when they kissed him. Some women loved it, insisting he never shave. He usually kept it short and trim. Her tender touch stoked the fire inside his heart, making the flames burn brighter. He wanted her to keep touching him.

"You're late for work." A crooked grin appeared on her lovely face. "I do know *your* schedule."

He chuckled. That she did. Over the past year, she would show up to demand answers on her sister's case at all hours of the day. Morning, noon, night. It wasn't always consistent, but she always arrived when she knew he'd be there. He shouldn't be surprised she learned his work schedule. Well, that he at least arrived to work at seven most days, unless a case called him in earlier.

She shifted again, just barely, but it was enough to give him another jolt of ecstasy straight to his cock. Her hand remained on his cheek and her eyes dilated with pleasure.

"You keep moving like that, Briella, and I won't be able to stop myself." Screw being late, and screw his captain and any ensuing berating he'd receive.

What was he thinking? God, he was an idiot. Why did he say that? He didn't have to be blunt and honest all the time. She was still hurting. He refused to be an asshole, yet he sounded like one.

"Maybe I don't want you to stop yourself."

The pressure on his cheek increased. He took it as his cue.

Okay, so they were going there. As much as he should stop what was about to happen, he couldn't find the energy to get out of bed. To ignore the desire building between them.

Lowering his head, his lips met hers. Softly and slowly— and so briefly, he wanted to shout and scream and stomp his feet.

He couldn't lose control. Not now. Not with her. She deserved better. The invisible line could not be crossed.

The internal war he waged with himself won the better part of his soul. The devil inside him wailed like a baby.

"We should talk."

Her hand fell as she turned her head away. "There's nothing to talk about."

"Well, no, there's a few things we need to talk about. One, how you're feeling today. Two, the reason why it bothered you I tried to put that alcohol away. Three, I just kissed you and I want to keep doing it. So, four, where does that leave us? Because, five, I'd like there to be an us." He exhaled, shocked he spoke so truthfully to her. Whoops. The devil was shifting the war.

But damn it. He wasn't lying. He wanted more with her. More of everything. Since he had declared his feelings, that meant he was done pussyfooting around everything, which meant he had to be honest. At all times. If he was going in, then he'd go all in. As Tate had said, screw the consequences. And there would be hell to pay if anyone found out he was messing around with someone involved in one of his murder cases.

Her eyes painstakingly took their time swiveling his way once again. "Okay, we'll talk. One, I'm fine. Two, I didn't mean to slap you and I apologize for it. Three, I might've wanted that kiss, but it shouldn't have happened. So, four, that leaves us where we always were. And five, there is no us."

He watched her eyes flash one emotion after another. She was so easy to read. He could even feel slight trembles now and again, her body giving away how nervous she was.

"I will never lie to you, Briella. I never have, and I don't plan to start now. I would appreciate the same courtesy. The only truthful thing you said was you're sorry for the slap and you wanted that kiss as much as I did."

"You're presuming you know me again. Like you know how I feel. Sorry to ruin your allusions and like you're this great catch, but I don't want you."

"Most women would've already gotten off my lap by now then. Yet, you're still sitting here." He couldn't help but add a devilish grin.

"I'm tempted to slap you again, Detective Stromberg."

"If it'll make you feel better, then so be it." His eyes softened as he brushed his hand up and down her back in a soothing caress. "You're hurting and you know it. If I have to be your punching bag, both verbally and physically, then I will be. I'd do anything for you."

She sucked in a sharp breath. Then her hand raised, and he swore for a second she was going to slap him again, but it landed on his cheek with a gentleness that made his heart skip a beat.

"You're going to make me cry again. Stop saying things like that to me."

"I can't help myself."

"You did for an entire year. You can keep doing it."

A wry grin split across his lips. "I nearly broke apart every single damn day keeping my feelings to myself. I can't say why they finally unleashed, but they did, and I won't take my words back. You can kick me out and I'll stay away," —his mind added *probably not* after that sentence—"but it won't stop how I feel about you."

Her gaze turned down, but her hand stayed pressed against his cheek as if that were the only thing anchoring her to reality.

"You have no idea..." Her voice cracked.

"Tell me what I don't know."

Her soulful eyes lifted. "I killed my sister. You can't love me because it's my fault. I killed her."

He swore his heart stopped beating as a rush of emotions slammed into him. Love? He never mentioned love, but damn, he was pretty sure he loved her. Did that mean she might love him in return with how she phrased it? He decided he'd ignore the love issue for now and focus on her asinine thinking that she killed her sister.

"I don't know why you think you killed your sister, but you didn't."

She shook her head and opened her mouth to respond, then clamped it shut. Her lips connected with his for no more than a second, and then she was out of his lap and standing a few feet away from the bed.

"Get out, Detective Stromberg."

Then why kiss him like that? Why give him another taste of her sweet lips? She didn't want him to leave.

But sometimes space was needed.

He nodded, disappointed she was running from him rather than fighting for what could be amazing between them. He should've known. Nothing had been easy with her from the first moment he met her.

He stood up. "I'll leave, but this isn't over."

"It is." She sounded firm in her decision.

"So, I'll never see you again?"

"Nope."

Well, he knew that was a damn lie. His cheesy grin said so.

And then it dawned on her. "Of course, you'll see me again. But only to inquire about my sister's case."

"Okay, then."

He had his work cut out for him, but he was ready to fight, even if she wasn't. Once he set his mind to something, there was no stopping him. Not even his job that he coveted.

He'd risk having her. He headed for her bedroom door and stopped before he twisted the knob, his back to her.

"I know this isn't an ideal time for any of this. I apologize if I hurt you because I couldn't keep my feelings to myself, but I hate seeing you in pain. I want to help you in any way I can."

Silence answered him. Did he expect anything different?

His hand twisted the knob.

"You did help me. You always do."

Damn. It was those tiny glimpses of how she felt that hurt the most. Especially when she refused to keep giving him more.

He was afraid to turn and ruin the moment. "Briella—"

"Call me Ms. Colton. Briella is too personal."

Oh, the nerve. He swiveled around, his brows low and his lips pressed together. She knew she had irritated him by the sweet, succulent smile spread across her lips. It was as if she were trying to incite a fight so he *wouldn't* leave, even though she had asked him to.

"Sorry, I only grant one request per day, and you asked me to leave, so I won't allow anymore...*Briella*."

Her face morphed into frustration. "You aggravate me... *Wyatt*."

Damn it. How did she know his first name? He shouldn't be surprised. Hell, she knew his work schedule too.

"If you know my first name, you know I'm not fond of it." Then he grinned. "But it doesn't sound half bad coming out of your sassy mouth."

Her lips twisted and turned as if she were trying hard to either hold in some nasty swear words or keep from smiling.

But he hadn't lied. It did sound pleasant on her lips. What would it sound like whispered in his ear as he thrusted deep inside her?

"Why don't you like it?"

Not something he wanted to get into right now. Nor did he have the time.

"I'll tell you later tonight."

She narrowed her eyes and crossed her arms, not happy with that answer.

"Good-bye, Wyatt. Get out."

He chuckled, deciding he'd let her have the last word. He grabbed the knob and opened the door. He got no more than a few steps down the hallway when the slashes of red across the wall that divided the living room from the kitchen pierced his eyes.

What the hell?

Briella must've noticed he stopped because he felt her presence behind him, and then her hand slipped into his.

"What...Wyatt?" Her frightened whispered words felt like a dagger to his heart.

He walked closer to examine what he hoped was only red paint.

You were supposed to be next.

Her grip tightened, crushing him to the bone.

"What does that mean? How didn't we hear anything?"

Both great questions.

He couldn't explain why he didn't hear anything. Maybe he had been so relaxed, enjoying how wonderful she felt in his arms, he hadn't been as focused as he should've been. Well, of course not. He hadn't heard his phone ring either, and it was dumb to think earlier that Tate hadn't called him.

But her first question had dread filling him up because he knew that answer.

The picture of the brutally mangled body pinned under the dripping paint—*please only be paint*—said it loud and clear.

Briella was supposed to die last night, not the nameless woman in the picture.

4

PICKING up the hot coffee cup, he took a sip. Then his lips curved up as the one person he'd been waiting for to arrive finally pulled alongside the curb and stepped out of his vehicle.

Detective Tate Powell. A jackass of great proportions. And Detective Stromberg's partner. They were two peas in a pod. Neither one cared who they railroaded, as long as they got their perp.

If he could put a bullet in their brains, he would. But that would be against the law, and he tried hard not to break the law. Sure, it happened on occasion—like Dawn's unfortunate murder—but he didn't make a habit of it. Plus, sometimes it helped to keep your enemies close.

And Detective Stromberg just climbed to the top of his enemy list.

How dare he touch her!

How dare he spend the night as if he had the right!

He was supposed to be with her last night. Comforting her. Consoling her.

He had had it all planned. The flowers were bought. The

strawberries all dipped in chocolate—by him, of course. A romantic poem that bespoke of his love and passion for her. He'd re-written it from the one he'd written for Dawn. That would be tacky to use the same poem, and he was *not* that kind of guy.

But no.

All his plans averted by that asshole detective, who couldn't mind his own business. Sure, Briella liked to hound him at his workplace, but he had no right to show up at her apartment and spend the night.

He hadn't been brazen enough to peek in the bedroom, so he had no idea what might've occurred between the two, but he could only assume they had sex. They. Were. In. Her. Bedroom.

His hand tightened on the coffee cup. He had to force himself to control his breathing and relax his hand before he crushed the cup and the contents spilled out.

It didn't matter.

None of it did.

Not Briella throwing herself into the detective's arms.

Not the detective overstepping his boundaries and daring to lay a hand on her.

Not the poor woman who had to die last night because he couldn't control his anger. As soon as he realized Briella wasn't alone, he left, intending to walk off his anger.

Except walking didn't do anything. Nothing helped. Until he saw her and heard her laugh. It had reminded him of Dawn's laugh. Sweet and delicate and filled with child-like wonder. Briella's laugh was a lot louder and more bois-terous, but it didn't totally grate on his nerves, so he over-looked it. Sometimes, when you loved someone, you had to overlook certain traits that weren't attractive. And for the most part, he found her very, very attractive. She was Dawn's sister, after all. He'd loved Dawn with a passion. Now that she was gone, it only seemed right—and fair to Briella—that he shift that love to her.

He had followed the woman home and slipped into her apartment without anyone noticing anything, not even her. Of course, he wasn't surprised. No one ever noticed him. He was invisible.

She took one look at him, and before she could even scream, he was on her. She died as Dawn had died—with the life draining from her eyes with a swiftness that surprised him.

He wasn't sure why. It wasn't the first time he took a life. But it had been a whole year. He assumed each death would be different, but it hadn't been.

Trying to control the anger simmering back to the surface, he pictured Briella's reaction to his little note on her wall.

After making sure he left not a scrap of evidence behind, he decided to pay Briella another visit. Her bedroom door had still been closed, and he sensed the detective behind it, so he didn't attempt to open it.

But he left them a little surprise.

You were supposed to be next.

A wry grin sprinkled across his lips before disappearing.

They thought he meant to kill Briella.

Not true.

He hadn't even meant to kill Dawn. It had been an accident. His anger had gotten the better of him. He regretted it, but there was no solace in regrets. So he got over it and moved his intentions toward Briella.

He loved her. As he loved her sister. And that's exactly what he meant to do last night. Confess his love. Show her how special and exquisitely beautiful she was. That he'd do anything for her.

She was supposed to be his girlfriend. Eventually wife. That's how much he loved Dawn. So, of course, he'd treat Briella with the same level of affection.

He had thought he was being kind giving her time to grieve. A whole year had been very generous of him. Plus, in a way, they had grieved together. He missed Dawn as well. And since he screwed up with Dawn, this was his chance to make it all right with Briella.

And she ruined it.

She ruined all of his plans.

It didn't matter.

It would all work out in the end.

Detective Stromberg would be busy finding out who the woman was—because he thought he'd be helpful leaving that tiny clue—and solving a murder. Which would leave him time to tell Briella everything.

How he felt.

How he loved her with all his heart.

How they'd live happily ever after.

And eventually, how he accidentally killed her sister.

SHE PACED BACK and forth in the kitchen, her gaze frequently gliding toward the cupboard where Wyatt had stashed her whiskey.

Wyatt...

She knew he didn't like his first name, which surprised her because she loved the sound of his name. Wyatt. Wyatt. Wyatt. After sweet-talking the officer who manned the front desk at his precinct, she had gotten tons of information about Wyatt. At first, to use anything and everything in her arsenal to light a fire up his ass to solve her sister's case. Somehow—she couldn't even remember exactly when—it turned into her just wanting to know more about him.

Like, why didn't he like his first name?

Although she knew he didn't care for it, she wanted to call him Wyatt from now on. It would help her keep him at a distance. And she definitely needed him to keep his distance.

Her steps slowed as she followed the same path from one end of the kitchen to the other as her eyes trained on the cupboard again.

Maybe one drink wouldn't hurt. It would drown out the murmurs she heard coming from the living room. Wyatt and Detective Powell were conversing about the horror slashed across her wall.

Maybe it would take the pain away for a brief, tiny moment.

Her stare was glued to the cupboard.

It would only take about five steps to walk around the small island separating her from her target.

No more than a few seconds to walk the distance, open the cupboard, then snatch the bottle. Wyatt wouldn't even be aware because she had some breath mints in her junk drawer near the same cupboard.

She twitched, ready to take a step, when a low-timbre voice stopped her.

"Don't even think about it."

Wyatt didn't hesitate to invade her space. He came so close to her that she tried to back up a step only to run into the counter.

"I have no idea what you're talking about."

His piercing blue eyes scorched her. "You know exactly

what I'm talking about. You want to go for that whiskey bottle. What will it solve?"

She tore her gaze away and stared intently at his chest. It rose up and down, as if his breathing and heart rate were going the same rapid tune as hers.

"How long will this take?"

A warm hand caressed her cheek. She couldn't stop herself from leaning into his soft touch. Why did he torture them both so much? "Depends how long it takes you to pack."

She flinched, her gaze whipping to his. "Excuse me?"

A wry, yet tired-looking smile graced his lips. "You honestly don't think I'm letting you stay here after what happened?" His brows rose in shock as he stared at her defiant expression. "Oh, wow. You did."

"And where exactly am I supposed to go?"

His hand still held her cheek, his thumb rubbing back and forth in a soothing motion. "Home. With me." His eyes narrowed, the intensity and the fire bursting like a fuse on dynamite. "You can argue with me all you want, but I'm not accepting the word no."

The deep part of her heart where she wanted to soak up every moment with this man screamed with joy. *Yes, take me home with you.* The other part of her frightened heart moaned with agony. *Stay the hell away from me.*

"We have a lot of work to do to find out who that woman is in the picture. But it says a lot, as does the message on the wall." He leaned closer, his lips a scant few inches from hers. "I will never let you get hurt. This bastard should've never even been able to get into your apartment. I failed you, and I refuse to fail again."

His breath smelled like peppermint, as if he had tossed in a mint at some point. Because he hadn't had a chance to brush his teeth or even shower. She had though. She couldn't stand to stare at the wall or wait for his partner to get to her apartment, so she had left the room and taken a quick shower and brushed her teeth. Her hair was still damp and uncombed. She didn't care how ridiculous she looked.

But with his mouth so close, the fresh smell so enticing, she did the only thing she had wanted to do since the last time he dropped all pretenses.

She kissed him.

His hand dropped from her cheek and encircled her waist. The kiss went from light and innocent to deep and intense. His tongue dove in, and she welcomed the intrusion. They explored each other as if searching for buried treasure. His hands tightened on her waist. She couldn't be sure if that was to stop himself from exploring more of her body or because the kiss was driving him wild.

She didn't care either way, but she never wanted it to end.

A throat cleared.

She flinched. Wyatt slowed the kiss and moved his mouth away. His hands stayed tethered to her like an anchor to a ship. His head glided toward his left where Detective Powell stood with an amused grin.

She felt her entire face heat up, probably as red as a tomato. She wanted to bow her head and bury herself in Wyatt's jacket from the embarrassment of getting caught kissing. Although she was a grown-ass woman. She could do whatever the hell she wanted with whomever she wanted.

Forcing herself to remain with that defiant attitude, she followed Wyatt's gaze and made eye contact with Detective Powell. She wasn't brave enough to actually speak though.

"Sorry to interrupt, but the crime scene crew is here. Thought you might want to know."

Wyatt nodded. "Thanks. You can get the hell out now."

"Yeah, sure. I don't mind waiting all by myself while you get it on in the kitchen."

She tensed. Not only embarrassed but uncomfortable.

"Now, jackass."

Detective Powell nodded. "Don't be too long, asshole." Then he walked out.

Wyatt rested against her body, fitting perfectly with her. She loved how solid and real and warm he felt. He made her feel safe and secure when a lot of the time she felt so lost and alone and, sometimes, even scared of her own shadow.

There had been no forced entry into her sister's apartment, which suggested she knew her attacker. Did that mean she knew the killer as well? The unknown terrified her, making her look over her shoulder more than she cared to admit. Not that she'd ever admit it out loud. Not even to Wyatt.

"I would love to continue what just happened, but we can't. Not right now." Pulling her into his embrace, squeezing her in a tender hug, she felt his lips touch the side of her head. "Please don't argue with me, Briella. Not about this. I'll keep my distance if you want me to—although that kiss said you don't want me to. Hell, I shouldn't touch you based on the fact you're now more involved in this case than I like."

"Meaning what?"

He frowned, and she wanted to smooth the wrinkles out of his forehead. "Meaning it's against protocol for me to be involved with a witness or anyone related to one of my cases. I could lose my job over this."

On that confession alone, she figured he would've

backed up and let go of her. If anything, his grip around her waist strengthened even more. He was tossing protocol—and his job?—right out the window. For her? Why? A few kisses shouldn't mean anything. They shouldn't make him want to risk his job.

"I need you to pack a bag and come home with me."

Yet, he was taking the risk. Screw the consequences. And there would be heavy, irrevocable consequences if anyone found out.

She had a feeling she'd regret this decision.

But being in his arms felt right.

And she couldn't resist him when he held her so intently, as if, if he let go, she'd slip away into the deep nether regions of the ocean never to be seen again.

"Okay, Wyatt. I'll come home with you."

Words he always wanted to hear.

I'll come home with you.

Although she had spoken it with such emotion, longing, and anticipation, she had been nothing but a pain in his ass as soon as he stepped away from her.

It wasn't as if he could keep her locked in his embrace all day long. He had a murder to solve—as soon as they found the body, that is.

Which was why they couldn't mess around. He watched her like a hawk as she packed a bag, itching to leave. He figured his domineering presence made her slow down in her task on purpose. To aggravate him. It took her forever to pick out a few outfits. He hadn't been sure how long she'd be staying with him when she asked the innocent question. He gave her a noncommittal, 'A few days.' He didn't want to say it would be too long and scare her off. But he also didn't want to say it would be too short and face her wrath when it turned into something longer. A few days would have to suffice. Honestly, he wasn't letting her out of his sight until this killer was caught.

At the rate he was currently going—a whole year with no leads—Briella would be moving in with him and never leaving.

And he had no problem with that scenario whatsoever.

Not that he planned to say anything of the sort to her.

Once she finally finished packing, he told Tate to start working on the case and he'd meet up with him soon. They had to find their victim. He had no doubts she was dead. Unfortunately, the paint on the wall was not paint at all. The sick bastard had written that disturbing message in blood. That poor woman. Violated. Murdered. Then treated even more callously when he smeared her blood to send Briella that threatening message. Hopefully, her death had been quick and semi-painless. Based on the picture alone, he knew she'd been stabbed too many times. Which meant it hadn't been painless. But he could still hope she hadn't felt much.

He drove Briella straight to his apartment. The tour was quick—a small one-bedroom place he barely saw because he worked so much—and then warned her not to open the door for anyone. He also told her not to tell a soul where she was, and better yet, just don't call anyone.

By the fierce frown plastered on her lips and the death glare beaming from her eyes, he irritated her once again with his demands.

Well, tough.

Someone wanted to hurt her, and he refused to let anyone touch her.

While he wanted to stay with her, comfort her, console her, get to know her more, he also had to work the case. He had to find the dead woman and the person responsible for two murders. Because, although he hadn't seen the actual crime scene yet, based on the picture, it mirrored Briella's sister's murder to a T. He was looking for the same killer. Why else would some random killer break in and post that message? Of course, he was looking for the same person who had murdered Dawn.

The question that bothered him was, why did he wait a year to come after Briella? On the anniversary of her sister's death? What kind of sicko did that?

He thought he had seen the worst of the worst with Cooper, Abby's brother who wreaked havoc on Tate and Abby's life how many months ago.

Boy, he'd been wrong. It could always get worse.

Before he changed his mind and stayed with her—he had a job to do, so he couldn't—he left her. All alone in his apartment.

But nobody would look for her there. He made sure when he drove to his apartment to take a very random route in case the killer had been watching her apartment. He couldn't be too careful right now, not when it came to her safety.

Hell, he had no intention of telling his captain or anyone else in the department where he'd stashed Briella. He trusted Tate to keep his secret. If his captain found out he brought Briella to his apartment...well, he wouldn't think about it because nothing good would happen.

Briella wasn't stupid. He trusted her not to leave or call anyone or do anything that would draw attention. He felt secure knowing she was in his domain, even though she was all alone.

He met Tate at the precinct where he was combing through calls coming through the emergency services line, hoping to find one that matched the crime scene they were looking for. The woman's face was too bloody to scan into facial recognition software, so no hope of identifying her that way. They just had to find a bit of luck that someone found her body already—or soon—and called the police.

"Anything?"

"Sorry, man. Not yet."

Stromberg sat down in his chair, deflated. Not that he expected a different answer. "It doesn't surprise me. Nothing about this case is simple."

Tate didn't need to ask what case he was referring to; he knew he was talking about Briella's sister. They had already hashed it out at Briella's apartment, albeit not too loud where Briella might've overheard. She was already teetering on the edge of destruction. The whiskey bottle, her cut hand, her entire behavior last night told him so.

"It's odd this killer waited an entire year." Tate's fingers stopped pounding on his keyboard as he leaned forward. "We've already established that Dawn probably knew the killer, which is why there wasn't any forced entry. It stands to reason Briella knows the dude too."

"It's not that simple," Stromberg said a little too sharply, leaning forward as well, mimicking Tate. His jaw clenched, his anger seething. "She didn't let anyone into her apartment last night besides me. We didn't hear a damn thing." He slammed his hand down hard on his desk.

Tate nodded, his expression softening, something that grated on Stromberg's nerves. He didn't want Tate's damn sympathy.

"It's not your fault." Tate sat back, running a hand through his unruly hair that needed a haircut. Something he kept yapping about but had yet to do. "Okay, so maybe we got it wrong. He broke into Briella's apartment last night without either of you the wiser. He could've done the same with Dawn, which means she didn't know her killer. Which would make more sense, considering you've run down every possible person she knew and cleared them as a suspect."

"Unless I missed something."

Damn it. He could've. He wasn't perfect. Briella bugging him about the case, in his face, the increasing pressure to solve it for her, could've made him rush and miss something.

That wasn't fair though. He couldn't blame Briella, as if she distracted him. If he made a mistake, it was because he screwed up somewhere.

But where?

"I can't discount anyone I previously interviewed or cleared. As of right now, anyone who knew Dawn—hell, who knows Briella—is a suspect. Once we find this new victim, we will cross-reference to see if they had a common friend or acquaintance. Either way, whether Dawn knew her killer or if it was some random jackass, this guy is good. We need to find him. Now."

This minute.

This second.

Because he was already a year too late.

If he would've found the killer as soon as Dawn's case hit his desk, this innocent woman who they now were searching for, would've never lost her life.

Her death was on his conscience.

It was his fault.

Tate's computer made a dinging noise.

His jaw loosened a fraction, although the tension and anger still simmered below the surface. He met Tate's gaze.

"This latest call looks like it could be a winner." Tate stood up and threw on his jacket.

"Let's hope so." He followed Tate's actions. "Because I can't look Briella in the eyes anymore and tell her I got nothing."

Yet, he feared that's exactly what would happen tonight when he got home.

5

IT DIDN'T TAKE LONG for Briella to get bored in Wyatt's apartment. Very, very bored.

And oh so curious.

Hence, her poking her nose in Wyatt's business. She searched every drawer, closet, room, even underneath the cushions, because who knew what he might hide and where. Sadly, she didn't find anything exciting or any juicy detail to hold over his head. Like a girlfriend she had no idea about.

Of course, not that she knew *everything* about him, but she knew enough after bombarding his space for over a year.

She didn't even know why it crossed her mind he might have a girlfriend. He hadn't lied to her once, not even when she had seen it in his eyes he didn't want to tell her for the thousandth time he had no new leads on her sister's case.

Maybe it was the part of her that had to make sure since she had been cheated on before. She didn't want to be the *other* girl in that kind of scenario. She certainly didn't like being the one who got cheated on, let alone be the cause of a breakup.

None of that mattered though. That guy wasn't even a blip on her radar anymore. She wasn't going to let something like that affect her. Okay, so she got cheated on. Only losers did that, and she didn't have time for losers. So she had moved on, except with more caution when it came to men. That didn't mean she didn't date. She was just more particular in who she dated and who she brought home.

But in the past year, no man entered her thoughts but Wyatt. Partly because she was still mourning her sister and so focused on finding some peace she didn't think she'd ever achieve. Partly because he intrigued her. He reeled her in with his determination and kindness.

Despite not finding anything to manipulate him with— because she had to guard her heart somehow—she learned he loved the sport of baseball. He also loved to collect coins —an odd hobby she never pictured him doing. And the most surprising was he had a sweet tooth. She had already eaten half the bag of gummy worms he had on his kitchen counter. Plus a few cookies from the pantry. And a couple handfuls of caramels from the jar near the fridge. It was either that or leave the apartment to indulge in the whiskey she couldn't last night. Wyatt only had beer in the fridge, and that sounded disgusting.

No matter how much the temptation sizzled through her veins, the strong pull, the deep ache in her gut to have a glass of whiskey burn down her throat, she resisted. She wasn't an idiot. It wasn't safe, and Wyatt would be pissed. The last thing she wanted to do was upset him when he had been nothing but caring and doing his best to find her sister's killer. Although the way he frowned, his brows pulling low, the slight irritation in his eyes made her heart pitter-patter erratically. He looked adorable angry at her. But that didn't mean she wanted to purposely make him mad.

After conducting her sleuthing, she made his bed. The covers were in a tangled mess. One pillow near the top and another near the edge of the bed on the opposite side. She couldn't determine whether he had to rush out of his apartment because he was running late, or he simply made a mess of his bed on a daily basis. But she had felt compelled to make it. Plus...boredom. She always made her bed. It helped her feel like her day was going to be okay because one thing was in order.

Because most days, her life was chaos.

No family. Sure, a few aunts and uncles she rarely spoke to. But otherwise, she had no family. She didn't have her sister. Her mom died of liver disease a few years ago. That's what overindulging in alcohol did to a person. A few years before that, her dad had died of a heart attack. Probably from the hell his wife had put him through. Despite the constant arguing and unpleasantness every single day, he never divorced her. That had been a rough time in her life. Losing her dad before her mom. Now they were both gone. So was her sister. She was all alone in the world. Each year, it's as if life wanted to throw her another curve ball. Keep making her life as difficult as it could possibly be.

She didn't have many friends. She had a lot before her sister died, even if she had moments of insanity when her parents died. She'd hung on to them as best as she could. She had loved to go clubbing, meeting new people, dancing the night away. Letting all the anguish disappear at the bottom of a bottle. She had always gone out with the same three girls. Opal, Lila, and Olive. They had so much fun together. They rarely had to wait in lines, they were so well-known in some parts of the city. One bartender at their favorite hotspot had even teased and shouted when he saw them arrive, "BOLO!" Be on the lookout. The first letters of their names. Briella, Opal, Lila, and Olive. It had been their little joke.

About a month after her sister had passed, Lila had sent a text. One word. BOLO. Bri had ignored it. She hadn't been ready. Hell, a year had passed, and she still didn't think she was ready.

Because she couldn't seem to make that connection with the people she used to hang out with every week, they stopped trying. They stopped calling. Her life kept getting lonelier and lonelier.

Her job even sucked. Working at a small diner that didn't serve the best food, even she could admit that. The tips usually teetered on pathetic because the food wasn't up to par, even though she worked her ass off giving the best service she could. Well, that's what she got for rolling through life like it was a joke. Skipping college, partying with friends. Acting like nothing bad could happen to her.

One night changed everything. When her parents died, she had accepted that was the way life went. Children usually surpassed their parents. But when her sister died...

Sinking onto the soft mattress in Wyatt's room, she inhaled deeply to hold back the tears she felt threatening to unleash. She would not cry. Not again. Not here. She refused to taint his place with sadness.

Yet, her mind always conjured bad memories. The idiotic mistakes she made. The wrong choices she could've made right with one decision in another direction.

Why did Wyatt even like her? She was pathetic. She couldn't hold a job for long, particularly in the past year because the grief became too much at times. Thankfully, her latest job at the diner was making its way to three whole months. That was a record for her. She had even asked for a week off, knowing the anniversary of her sister's death would hit her hard. Although her boss failed at cooking, he had a decent heart and didn't argue or deny her request. Much better than the asshole she worked for when her sister had been murdered.

She had an entire week to herself, but not anymore. Circumstances had yet again thrown her for a loop. Took her life off track and into a reality she didn't know if she'd survive.

Yes, Wyatt was a good man.

Yes, he tried his damndest to find her sister's killer.

Oh, yes, she liked him more than she should.

But no, opening her heart would bring nothing but... heartache. Because if life had taught her anything, it was heartache always followed, no matter how hard she tried to find happiness.

She jumped when a loud knock echoed down the short hallway.

Damn. Someone was at the door.

Wyatt told her not to answer the door for anyone. Not to call anyone. Not to do anything but wait for him to get home.

Another knock sounded, followed by a muffled voice. She couldn't make out much, considering she hadn't moved from her spot on his bed.

Deciding she wouldn't let anything scare her, she stood up and headed for the front door with purposeful steps. Just because someone knocked on the door and she was walking toward it like she was on a mission didn't mean she'd actually open it.

One more knock sounded. Light, unthreatening. Followed by a gentle voice. A woman.

"Briella, I know you're in there. Please open the door."

She didn't recognize the voice, but whoever it was knew she was here. How? And why?

Peering through the peephole, trying to be quiet as a mouse with her movements, she jumped back when she saw who it was.

STROMBERG CIRCLED the woman's body, swallowing back the bile that made its way up and nearly out of his mouth. Turning his gaze away, he breathed through his mouth, trying to find his composure. He hadn't thrown up at a crime scene since he was a newbie detective. Years ago, and it had only happened once. His first crime scene ever. It had been a small boy who had fallen into a pond in Central Park and drowned before his parents even knew he disappeared into the water. It had been a sad, senseless death. He had purged the disgust from his body, then pushed his emotions aside and did his job. Something he needed to do right now.

"You've walked around her body at least ten times now. Nothing changed since the last round you made."

Tate's irritating voice made him stand up and back away. He was right, of course. He had looked at the dead woman —Flora Johnson, age twenty-six, single—until his eyesight blurred and his mind told him he'd go crazy if he didn't look away. Yet, if he stopped, how would he find the evidence he needed to find this bastard?

The killer had been savage. Multiple stab wounds littered across her body. From head to toe. Across her face.

Down her torso. Along her thighs. And the wounds between her legs painted a very brutal picture.

Just like Dawn.

A mirror image of the crime scene. Right down to the way the body was positioned on the bed.

He had no doubt he was looking for the same killer. As if the pinned picture and dripping blood running down the wall in Briella's apartment wasn't enough of a clue.

Looking at Tate, his stance stiffened as his brows fell into a deeper frown. "I'll circle her another twenty times if it helps find this bastard."

Tate's eyes reflected the same passion as was inflicted in his voice. "Oh, we'll find him. But you're not doing anything but torturing yourself by glaring hard at her body. Let's let the crime scene crew do their thing and work the case. We found the body. We have somewhere to go from here. We should be thankful we found her so quickly. We have no idea if this jackass thought it'd take us longer, but we're good." Tate stepped closer to him and grabbed him by the shoulders. "We're the best. We got this. We'll get him."

When Tate said it so passionately, Stromberg believed him.

But he had a whole year to get this killer, and he didn't. What made it different now? Because based on their preliminary search of the crime scene, they didn't have much evidence to go on. Exactly like Dawn.

"You want an award for that epic speech?"

Tate chuckled and slapped him on the back. "Biggest damn one you can find. That's my partner. That's the asshole I want to see. Let's get out of here and interview some of Flora's neighbors."

Stromberg couldn't help but laugh with him and then nodded. Tate was right, of course, the jackass. Always right.

They gave a stern warning to the head of the crime scene crew to call them immediately if they found anything and then left the apartment. They'd already talked to her neighbor down the hallway, Courtney. She had called 9-1-1 when she found Flora's body. They didn't live in a terrible neighborhood, but it also wasn't the best. They'd met a year ago and had formed a friendship. They looked out for each other. When Courtney got a call from Flora's co-worker she hadn't shown up for work, she let herself in with the key Flora had given her and found her body. Flora had one for Courtney's apartment as well. Thank goodness for small favors that it hadn't taken forever for her murder to be detected.

Stromberg started on the left side of the hallway, knocking on doors, asking questions, while Tate worked the right side.

They met at the end, about thirty minutes later, with some helpful information to lead them in a new direction.

Flora lived alone. Rarely had visitors. No boyfriend they were aware of. She was polite but quiet. She worked around the corner at the laundromat in the mornings, and according to Courtney, also worked at a bar as a waitress three nights a week. Her parents lived out of state in New Jersey. They took a few minutes to make the call no detective —or officer—wanted to make. The news of death. But for this situation, they called the local precinct where the parents lived and asked them to do it. Receiving the news was always better in person than over the phone.

Stromberg took point on it, requesting the detective to ask certain questions after they delivered the brutal news. An hour later, the detective informed him she left home three years ago for the big city and never looked back. She didn't even say why she wanted to leave or why she picked

New York. They hadn't talked to their daughter in over a year. They had no idea what she had been up to.

So far, Flora was full of more questions than answers. She appeared to be a recluse, although working hard to make money. Why had she moved away from her family and friends? Why to such a big city? Why didn't she have many friends here other than Courtney?

All the questions bothered Stromberg. Questions about Flora and her decision-making. Questions why she had been the next victim of a madman. Questions of how she tied into Dawn. Because although the crime scenes matched, their backgrounds differed.

Dawn grew up in New York City. She had a good job, close to her sister and friends. No boyfriend, however.

They visited the laundromat where they spoke to her boss. The man sported a pot belly, stinky breath from smoking too much—a cigarette dangling from his mouth as they talked—and a penchant for a wandering eye.

"Mr. Becker, can you focus, please?" Tate asked for the third time, rolling his eyes.

Mr. Becker's gaze trailed to a young woman wearing tiny shorts and a tight tank top over by the top-loading washing machines in the corner.

Mr. Becker inhaled a long pull of his cigarette and then blew out the smoke, not taking care what direction he blew it in. Stromberg wanted to slap the cigarette out of his hand, then knock a fist into his face for being a disgusting pervert.

Which prompted his mind back to the crime scene. Dawn's and Flora's. They had both been raped. Both held down with brute strength, bruises marring their wrists, yet no indication they were able to fight their attacker. No skin or blood or any kind of DNA had been found underneath their fingernails to suggest they even got a scratch or hit in to defend themselves. Mr. Becker was a large man. Although fat in the belly, his arms carried plenty of muscle.

Stromberg made a mental note to cross-check if Dawn ever came around this area. To this laundromat.

"How long has Flora worked for you?" Tate asked again.

Mr. Becker shrugged. "Two, three months." He took another drag from his cigarette. "Uh, maybe it's been five. The months all roll together so fast. Poor Flora. She was a pretty gal. Good worker. I was pretty pissed this morning when she didn't show up."

Thankfully, Flora's co-worker, another woman who had looked wary of Mr. Becker when they arrived—rightly so—had called her neighbor to check on her. Flora wasn't known to not show up without calling in about it.

Stromberg couldn't stop from rolling his eyes, mimicking Tate from moments ago. This guy. What an asshole. "Any problems with her?"

Mr. Becker looked at him as if *he* was the idiot. "I just said she was a good worker."

"You also said you were pissed she didn't show up. Do you get upset a lot?"

Smoke filtered in his direction as Mr. Becker's expression turned from bored to alert in seconds. "I don't. But I was frustrated this morning, so yeah, I got pissed when I got a call Flora didn't show up. Obviously, I know why now."

"Why were you frustrated?" Tate asked as if he were asking what he wanted for his birthday.

"None of your damn business." He drew another quick drag from the cigarette, then snuffed out the butt in an over-filled ashtray sitting on the counter. "Am I suspect for some reason? I don't like the tone you two are using."

Stromberg had enough. He lost it. He grabbed Mr. Becker by the front of the shirt and shoved him against the wall. Leaning in close, he regretted that decision when the stale smell of cigarettes coated his nostrils. "And I don't like perverts or assholes that hurt women."

Mr. Becker's brows puckered low, mean and menacing. "Well, I ain't neither. So get your damn hands off me."

He'd do what he damn well pleased. If this asshole hurt Flora or Dawn, he'd pay. He'd regret the day he broke into Briella's apartment and slashed that disgusting message on her wall.

"Respectable business owner like you, I would never think of you like that." Tate's words floated in the air as if tension wasn't filling the room like a blazing fire had just been unleashed from an unattended cigarette. As if Stromberg didn't have the man pressed up against the wall with no probable cause to do so. "Where were you last night?"

Mr. Becker blinked rapidly. Like he was trying to decipher whether Tate was on his side or not. "At home. Tell your damn partner to let me go. I'll file harassment charges against the both of you!"

Tate smiled and leaned casually against the counter. "Anyone with you?"

"No." His answer was short and clipped, his eyes still narrowed into tiny slits.

"Well, I guess we're done here." Tate laid his business card on the counter. "Please call me if you think of anything important we should know. We want to find who killed Flora as much as I'm sure you want us to find the person too."

Stromberg figured that was his cue to let the asshole go, but he didn't want to. He wanted him to confess to everything and this nightmare to be over with. Tate's short tap on his shoulder said it was time though.

He shoved Mr. Becker as he let go and took a few steps back. "Stop ogling the women in here. Don't be a damn pervert."

Mr. Becker rearranged his shirt, smoothing his hands down the front of it. "You'll be hearing from my lawyer."

Stromberg looked around the room, no doubt assuming there'd be a few health violations he'd find if he really looked. Like smoking inside the building. Did Mr. Becker own the building or rent it? He imagined the landlord wouldn't appreciate someone smoking on the premises. Talk about a fire hazard.

"Good." Stromberg smiled with the devil flashing in his eyes. "You'll need one. I can already see a few violations going on in this building to get you shut down. Not to mention the whole murder thing. Angry at the victim. Disgusting pervert. You make a nice suspect."

That had Mr. Becker's eyes widening, then shuffling on his feet as if thinking of a good comeback.

"I'll be waiting for the call." Stromberg turned around and headed outside, inhaling the fresh air and trying to get the disgusting cigarette smell out of his nose.

"We need to look into him more," he said as soon as Tate joined him on the sidewalk.

"Oh, definitely. I wouldn't go there with my laundry if I was a woman. I can't imagine why Flora even worked there." Tate grabbed the passenger car door. "What the hell was that back there?"

He slammed his door shut, ignoring the berating from Tate. Like he'd never gotten into a suspect's face before. The audacity to ask him such a stupid question.

Tate's door slammed just as hard. "Hello, I asked you a damn question."

"Your question didn't deserve a response. It's stupid! But,

okay, here you go. I was interviewing a potential suspect. I don't like that asshole."

"And that asshole could report you for police brutality."

Whatever. Tack on another mark against him for breaking protocol. He was so good at it lately.

Tate sighed. "Do you want to check in on, Briella? Would that calm you down so you don't rough up any more people we decide to interview?"

Hell, yeah. He'd been worrying about her since the moment he left. She was alone. In his apartment.

That didn't mean he'd calm down at all. He needed answers, and he was done asking nicely for them.

He'd take Tate up on his offer. It couldn't hurt to check on her.

"Just a quick stop. Make sure she's okay."

Tate chuckled. "I'll even wait in the car so you can kiss her without an audience."

Jackass.

Of course, he'd stay in the car.

Because he damn well wasn't leaving her without kissing her at least once.

For his own peace of mind. To make sure she was okay.

Nothing more.

Not because he missed her sweet lips and delectable body close to his.

6

PLACING a hand over her mouth to stifle the loud laughter that wanted to escape, it slipped out anyway when she saw her companion's expression.

They both giggled hysterically.

"Oh my God, stop. You're going to make me pee in my pants. I have to use the bathroom." Bri stood up, embarrassed those words came out of her mouth, but it was the truth. She had to pee, and the laughing wasn't helping her bladder.

"Of course. I'll fill up our glasses."

Bri nodded, rounded the couch, and stopped when she heard a tiny click. Her eyes zoomed to the door as the handle turned. Her heart pounded as she watched in slow motion as the door swung open. She had no chance to react. To run forward and stop the door from opening.

But when her eyes landed on the person walking through the threshold, she let loose some more laughter at her ridiculousness.

"Wyatt, you're home already." Although her moment of panic had abated, the erratic beating of her heart increased.

Why *was* he home so early? Did he find something? Did he arrest her sister's murderer already? Did she have to leave? Was he going to kick her out immediately?

Question after question flooded her mind. Like a horror movie reel going in fast-forward. The knife slashing down over and over in rapid succession.

"Just stopping by to check on you." His eyes zoomed to her new friend sitting on the couch.

Oh, dear.

He was pissed, and if the furious frown marred on his face was any indication, he was more than pissed.

"What the hell are you doing here, Abby?" Then his gaze zoomed to her like a heat-seeking missile. "I thought I told you to not open the door for anyone."

She bit her bottom lip, unsure of what to say. Sure, they had gotten into it before. Mostly her rage displayed rather than his. But she had never seen him this upset.

"Oh, stop, Stromy. I didn't think it would hurt if I stopped by and checked on her. Don't get your panties in a twist," Abby said as she rounded the couch herself. "Where's Tate?"

"Waiting in the car," he replied dryly, his anger deflating a fraction. "What are you doing here? And you know I hate it when you call me Stromy."

"I just told you. I know you're not deaf." Then she grinned wickedly. "It's what friends do. Make nicknames for each other."

He inhaled deeply, running a hand through his hair. "Fine. *Why* are you here?"

Abby's brows puckered together. "I'm pretty sure that's the same question only worded differently. But maybe you didn't clean your ears this morning. I'm here checking on your girlfriend Briella. She experienced something traumatic and has a maniac after her. I was trying to be nice. Geez."

Abby rolled her eyes as she stepped closer to him. Patting his shoulder, she gave him a sympathetic smile. "I'm going to go say hi to Tate. Be gentle with her. She doesn't deserve your anger because you're scared."

Then Abby walked out of the apartment.

Girlfriend?

Was that how Wyatt saw her? As his girlfriend?

His gaze slowly met hers. His eyes mirrored the same confusion that echoed out of hers.

"I have to go to the bathroom." Then she fled the room.

She didn't want to decipher the confusion lingering between them. He couldn't see her as a girlfriend. They barely knew each other. Besides bombarding his life every few weeks about her sister's case, they didn't interact. Last night was an anomaly. Abby word-vomited without thinking about what she was saying.

Going to the bathroom, she took her time with everything, especially when it came to washing her hands. She didn't want to go back out there.

A soft knock sounded on the door.

"Are you okay?"

Gripping the sink, her eyes glossed over as she stared at herself in the mirror as his simple question lingered in the air.

Black circles coated her eyes. Her hair was a bit messy as she had been toying with it as she conversed with Abby. She looked like an utter horror compared to her usual put-together self. She might not be in a good place emotionally, but she usually tried to project she was.

"Briella?" Another gentle knock joined his low tone.

Why did he have to sound so concerned?

"I'm fine. I'll be right out."

She stood staring at herself until her hands ached from clutching the sink so hard for so long. Letting out a deep breath, she backed up and walked to the door, not exactly ready to face him, but knowing she couldn't hide in the bathroom forever.

Her hand twisted the knob and opened the door. She jumped back when Wyatt's crystal-blue eyes zoomed to hers. He stood leaning against the wall in the tiny hallway. As soon as their gazes connected, he straightened.

"I'm sorry I got upset. I didn't mean to hurt your feelings if I did."

Ugh. The man had to keep inching under her defenses with his sweetness. Why did he have to be so kind and considerate of her feelings?

She nodded, accepting his apology with a gesture instead of words. She didn't trust herself. Tears hovered near the edge. She'd cry again if she opened her mouth to respond.

He took a step closer. "I know Abby is Tate's fiancé, and I trust her. The three of us have been through a lot together. I trust both of them with my life. What I don't understand is why you opened the door when I told you not to. How do you even know her?"

Odd man. He apologized, then in the next breath, reprimanded her. Which he had every right to do. She had promised not to open the door for anyone.

"I met her once at the precinct. I knew she was Tate's fiancé. I didn't think you'd mind if she came inside."

He took another step. "I mind."

She frowned. "But she's your partner's fiancé?"

"But you promised not to open the door to anyone. It doesn't matter who she is."

"You don't trust her?"

His gaze lifted to the ceiling as if thinking about the question, then he lowered his gaze to hers, taking another step closer. One more step and he'd be able to wrap her in his arms. She wanted it so badly, yet she knew she shouldn't want anything from him, least of all his compassion.

"Were you not listening? I just said I trust her. I trust Tate like I've never trusted anyone in my life."

Why? She knew something happened with the three of them, yet she didn't know all the details. Five months ago, he had disappeared for about a week or so on a case he had been working on. Then Tate became his partner out of the blue, and she could tell right away there was some serious history between them. No matter how many times she questioned Officer Stiner at the front desk for details, he never confessed anything but the minor details. They had both been involved in a gunfight. Tate got shot. The perp had died. That was all he'd ever give her whenever she asked.

She closed the distance before he could, setting a hand on his chest. His heart thumped steadily, not even close to an erratic pace like hers. Pumping overtime at the tension building between them. Not just irritation, but the physical kind too.

"What happened? Why do you trust him so much?"

Wyatt lifted his hand and caressed her cheek as his other hand settled on her waist. "We were looking for a serial killer. I didn't trust Tate in the beginning. He was hiding something from me, and I hate liars. But we found our bad guy. Came face-to-face with him. It came down to us or him, and we won the fight. Barely."

"Same story I always hear. But it's not the whole story." While he hated liars, so did she. Not that he was necessarily lying to her, but he wasn't sharing everything, and she wanted it all. Unfair of her to even want such a thing, but when she was this close to him, she didn't care how unfair anything was, as long as she got her way. And maybe for him to stay as close as he could possibly be.

He grinned. "And how do you know this story?"

She matched his grin. "Being informed of your whereabouts is crucial to me when I need to bother you about my sister's case. You disappeared for a while a few months ago, and I needed to know why."

A low masculine chuckle floated between them. "Why am I not surprised?"

"So?"

His eyes crinkled, coated with indecision. The hand on her waist tightened as his other hand holding her cheek brushed lightly against her skin one more time. "Abby's brother was the serial killer we were looking for."

Wow. Not what Bri expected to hear.

Wyatt continued, "Cooper, Abby's brother, killed Tate's sister. Abby found out, and it created some difficulties because she didn't know what to do. In the end, it worked out. Not for Cooper, but for everyone else it did. Those two might not have a perfect relationship, but it's a strong one. They've been through a lot."

The way his eyes glittered with desire said he was saying more than what his words implied.

"How did she...how did she process all of that?"

A sad, tired grin split his lips. "She ran. She ran from Tate when it wasn't what he wanted. Even though she loved him. She thought it was the best decision."

"But they're together now."

He nodded. "Because they're meant to be together." His mouth lowered and his whispered words tore through her heart and splintered her soul. "I think we're meant to be together."

Then he kissed her.

HE WAS the dumbest man alive, but he couldn't have stopped the words even if he tried. He honestly believed they were meant for each other. Now all his dumb words would do was send her running for the hills. Not that he wouldn't fight her tooth and nail to stay with him.

The kiss deepened as the rightness of her in his arms strengthened his resolve that he was correct.

How many times did he count down the minutes to when she'd storm the precinct and get in his face? She usually came on the same day, every few weeks. Sure, the times differed, but she usually came on the same day. How many times did he dream about her at night wondering how she was coping? Was someone there to comfort her? Did she have a boyfriend? Things he wanted to know, yet didn't have the guts to ask. He had no right. He was only a detective working on her sister's case.

But now...

Now he was more. Since the first time her sweet lips met his.

A low, aching moan slipped from her as his hands tightened around her lithe body. When he held her like this, kissing her as if he were a dying man, he could feel the same pulsating desire coming from her.

It was always when they parted that the feeling went away and he could feel her slipping from his grasp.

Of course, he didn't know how long Abby would stay downstairs with Tate, and he had a murderer to find. The sooner he found his perp, the faster he could explore the relationship blooming between them with no interruptions.

Slowing the kiss, trying to explain how much he cared about her in each soft caress of his lips, he hated himself when he pulled his mouth away from hers. He felt the exact moment when the damn wall protecting her heart flew back up between them. Her eyes shuttered, masking her emotions, except for the irritation that he dared to kiss her again.

"You should stop kissing me."

A sly grin emerged. "I can't help myself."

She couldn't help herself either because a sweet, gorgeous smile appeared. "Well, try harder."

"Do you want Abby to stay when I leave?"

He felt terrible for changing the subject, but he had to leave, even though he'd rather stay right where he was. Holding the most precious thing in the world.

Her brows puckered together as her lips pressed into a thin line. "Oh, I have a choice? Because just moments ago you made it sound like I don't."

He chuckled. "Well, she's here now. I don't mind that she's here." His brows drooped low. "However, I don't like that you opened the door after you said you wouldn't."

She looked chagrined for her actions. "I looked through the peephole before I opened the door. And she sounded very determined, like she wouldn't leave unless I opened it up. I knew she was Tate's fiancé."

"That's not the point. I don't care who is on the other side, you don't open the door unless it's me."

He knew he was digging his heels in on this, being a bit too overbearing about it. But he couldn't risk losing her. Not to a madman that brutally tortured and raped his victims.

He would never survive if something that heinous happened to Briella.

"What happens if it's your partner Tate? I can't even open the door to him?"

Oh, she was testing his limits. What a damn hard question. He trusted his life with Tate. Sure, in the beginning, when he first met him, he didn't trust him worth a damn. He knew Tate had been hiding something. The fact he knew who the killer was, that it was his girlfriend's brother, and that that same man had killed his sister. He had been out for revenge. Not justice.

But in the end, Tate did the right thing. He took the higher road. They had been in a gunfight that had scared the living shit out of him. Not much scared him. He had seen a lot on the job. Evil people. Terrified people. Stupid people. Even though that hadn't been the first time to see the barrel of a gun staring him down, he had been scared shitless that his life was about to end.

Now, he and Tate didn't keep anything from each other.

"Wyatt? Why aren't you answering me? It can't be that hard of a question."

But she was wrong. It was more than difficult to take such a simple question and find an answer. He did not want her to open the door to anyone, even Abby. But did that include his partner he trusted with his life?

"No, I don't want you to even open the door up to Tate. I said no one, and I mean it."

"So, you don't trust him?"

He shifted in his spot, but he didn't remove his hands from her waist. Surprisingly, she hadn't made him let go yet. "I trust him. You can trust him. But it's simpler to say don't open the door to anyone."

That garnered another beautiful smile before she finally

extracted herself from his arms. "Fine. I promise I won't do it again. If Abby would like to stay, since she's already here, I'd like the company."

Keeping his pained groan to himself that she pulled away, he nodded. "I'll try not to be too late, but we're making headway."

"Yo, you ready?" Tate hollered down the hallway. Although, when Stromberg looked in the direction his voice came from, he didn't see him.

He hadn't even heard the front door open. And he was confused by the slight stiffness in Tate's voice. Had he and Abby argued about something? Maybe the fact she showed up here without telling either of them. But that was the thing about Abby. She did what she wanted regardless of the consequences.

"Come on." He grabbed her hand, needing a small connection with her, and pulled her down the hallway. "I'll explain more."

He found Tate by the couch, standing close to Abby. His expression indicated he was pissed. And for some reason, the vibes he was getting said Tate was pissed at him. What the hell did he do? Did Abby complain he yelled at her? He wouldn't exactly say he yelled, but he had a tone with her for sure. She pissed him off. She endangered Briella and forced her to make a decision she shouldn't have had to.

"I'm almost ready. You okay?"

"Fine."

Oh, yeah. Tate was upset. His clipped response didn't need any more words to get the drift he had done something.

Briella tugged on his hand. "You said you were making headway. What does that mean?"

Rather than taking his time to meet her gaze because he

didn't want to talk about it, he met her eyes head-on. "We found the woman from the picture. Flora Johnson. Do you know her?"

Briella looked disappointed as she shook her head. "The name doesn't ring a bell."

He pulled out his phone and scrolled until he found a picture of Flora. The one from her driver's license, since her face now was marked with knife wounds. He showed Briella, who again shook her head.

"She worked at a laundromat near her apartment. Suds-n-Wash. Ever been there? Your sister?"

Briella sighed. "No, I've never been there. As far as I know, Dawn never used a laundromat. I can't be one hundred percent certain though."

He hated the disappointment in her voice, as if she ruined any possible leads. It wasn't her fault. None of this was. Not her sister's death. Not his lack of finding evidence. Not even this maniac gunning for her now.

"I'm glad you found her." Briella's eyes were turned down as if she couldn't even bear to look him in the eye for her failures. "No evidence? I hope there's something this time."

Touching her chin, he raised it until her golden depths met his. Her desolate look pierced his heart with an ache so strong, he wanted to cradle her in his arms and walk out of the room and hold her. Remove the pain and replace it with something happier. "I will find this bastard. He won't get away. None of this is your fault."

Her bottom lip wobbled, and her eyes filled up with water, yet not one tear made an entrance.

A snap of fingers jolted him out of the trance Briella had pulled him into. He looked at Abby, who appeared excited.

"I think I know her." Abby shrugged, yet the excitement

was still displayed. "I mean, I know a Flora. She works at a bar I've been to. We chatted a few times. She might've worked at a laundromat. I don't remember everything about her."

"Seriously?" Tate groaned as he ran a hand down his face. "Your phone, asshole."

Stromberg rolled his eyes at the irritation lingering in Tate's voice. He handed Tate his phone and waited as Abby took a look at Flora Johnson's picture.

She tapped the screen, her eyes shining with delight. "Yep. That's her." Then her expression turned downward, her eyes filled with a deep ache he felt to his bones. "She was so sweet. I can't believe she's dead."

"What bar did she work at?" he asked, wondering if it would match the same bar the neighbors gave them.

"Gunner's Bar."

It was a match.

"When the hell have you been in that neighborhood?" Tate demanded.

Yeah, Stromberg was also curious, although he would've never asked. It wasn't his business what Abby did. But it wasn't a pretty neighborhood. Gangs ruled the streets, and venturing out at night by yourself was never safe, especially for a woman.

Abby cocked a brow and slapped a hand to her hip. "Before you found me. And if I wanted to go there now, you couldn't stop me."

"Wanna bet?" Tate growled with a threatening tone. "You will never step foot in that bar again. In that neighborhood again."

"Don't you tell—"

Tate cut her off when he grabbed her cheeks and leaned

in closer. "I can't lose you. Those three months apart were the worst days of my life. I wouldn't survive without you."

Abby closed the distance and kissed him. "I won't go there. I have no reason to now. But you also can't tell me what to do."

He let go of her, yet narrowed his eyes. "We'll talk about this later."

She grinned deviously.

Stromberg had no desire to see any more of their interaction. First, because they had a case to solve and a killer to find. Second, because it hurt for the first time to see their love so blatantly when he feared he'd never get that far with Briella.

"Anything you remember about her? Anything that sticks out?"

Abby looked contemplative. They all waited in silence. "She was always friendly. Great memory. Knew my drink without asking."

Tate groaned low. Because that indicated Abby ventured to the bar quite often if the bartender had memorized her drink.

Stromberg cleared his throat to keep them on track.

Abby sent Tate a dirty, mischievous smile, then continued. "The other bartender there. He was friendly. He was also a little grabby with her. Slapped her ass here and there. Liked to touch her hair and put it behind her ear. Flora didn't stop the behavior, but she also didn't seem to like it."

"You remember his name?" Tate asked tight-lipped.

"Nick." She tossed her shoulder up in a careless gesture. "I'm sorry, but I don't know any of their last names. But his first name was Nick."

"It's a good place to start. Thank you, Abby. We should

go." Stromberg directed his attention to Tate, who nodded and then dismissed him without further ado.

Damn. What could've pissed him off?

Turning his attention to Briella, he framed her face, and before she could step away, he pressed his lips to hers. Nothing intense, but enough to show her he'd miss her. That he'd be thinking about her. That he couldn't wait to come home and spend the night with her.

"Don't open the door."

She smiled, but he saw the tiredness, the ache in her golden depths. "I won't. And you be safe."

"Always."

They left his apartment. He made sure to lock the door behind him and didn't say a word to Tate until they walked into the elevator.

"Okay, man. What the hell? You seem pissed."

Tate jabbed the ground floor button. "Yeah, well, when you think you know someone and then come to find they're not your friend."

He twisted toward Tate and waited until he finally looked at him. "What does that mean?"

The hatred pouring from Tate's gaze gutted him. "I heard you." His eyes narrowed. "I heard you tell Briella not to open the door even if I showed up. So much for trust between us."

Tate swiveled his direction forward.

Damn.

It didn't have anything to do with trust. At least, not on Tate's side. He didn't want to put Briella in an uncomfortable position where she had to remember who she could open the door up to and who she couldn't. Why not eliminate all confusion and say don't open it to anyone?

"You didn't hear the part where I told her I trusted you. I

want to make it easy on her. Don't open the damn door to anyone."

The elevator door swung open. Tate looked at him. "This is why I don't do partners."

Then he walked out without glancing behind him.

Well, shit.

The last thing he wanted to do was offend and hurt his friend. Not what he needed right now.

Shoving the pain aside that he lost his best friend, he focused on what was most important.

Finding the killer intent on harming Briella.

7

BRIELLA PLOPPED down on the couch next to Abby, who grinned sheepishly at her. "Sorry about that. I didn't mean to upset Stromy."

Briella shrugged, unsure of the right words to say. They weren't exactly friends where she thought she could be completely honest, especially her real feelings for Wyatt. Of course, maybe Abby knew how much she liked him. She didn't exactly push him away when he kissed her in front of them.

And it wasn't Abby's fault he was so pissed. It was hers. Although she had felt comfortable and safe opening the door to Abby, she hadn't listened to him. She upset him, and she'd accept the blame for it.

"Do you want me to leave?"

She looked at Abby, making sure to smile, even though she didn't feel like it. "No, I don't. I don't know if I'll be good company now, but I don't think I want to be alone."

Abby laid a gentle hand on her arm and squeezed. "I know I didn't say it earlier because I'm not good with emotions and crap, but I am sorry about your sister. About what's going on right now."

"Thank you." Bri could relate to the whole not good with emotions and crap. Her sister was always on her case for ignoring how she felt and not talking to her about, well, anything. Like the guy she had been dating when her sister had been murdered. It took her sister's death to finally realize what a complete douche he had been. Something her sister tried to tell her. Of course, not something she wanted to think about right now because it brought back memories of that night. A night she wanted to erase from her memories.

Abby cleared her throat and moved her hand back to her lap. "So. You and Stromy?"

"What about us?" Ugh. Not what she meant to say. "Not that there is an us. There's not. I mean, what about me and him?"

Abby smiled and then laughed. "Oh, there is an *us* between you two. Umm...he kissed you before he left."

Bri averted her eyes. Not a conversation she wanted to have, but it was better than the memories forming in her mind. "Yeah, he shouldn't have."

"I have a hard time picturing him with anyone, he's always so gruff and serious, which is why I love calling him Stromy. It helps remove that gruffness," Abby said. "But you two look good together. He likes you."

Yeah, she didn't need to be told that. His kisses said enough. And oh, how she wanted more kisses.

What would happen tonight when he got home?

Nothing.

That's what should happen. Absolutely nothing. Because she didn't deserve anything sweet and good in her life, not when her sister couldn't have the same thing.

"Briella?"

She sighed heavily. How did she put into words how she felt? Her thoughts on the whole matter. "It would never work between us."

That's the best she could do. Because delving any deeper, it'd bring her to the dangerous territory of thinking about her sister.

"I thought the same thing for a while about me and Tate. I couldn't understand how we'd overcome the fact my brother killed his sister and how I didn't want him to kill my brother."

Bri slowly met Abby's gaze. Because wow. How did a person address something so heavy? "So, how did you overcome it?"

Abby swallowed, then looked away. "I'm not sure, to be honest. I'm still working on it. My brother ended up dying and that was that. I ran away though. In the beginning. I thought he'd be better off without me. I mean, my brother was a serial killer. He killed Tate's sister. How could he love me?"

"But he does." The one time Bri saw them at the precinct, she saw the love clearly between them. It had made her insanely jealous. Because she knew she'd never have anything close to something that precious. She'd been spying on them too. Soaking it all up. She was pretty sure she'd been extra mean to Wyatt that day because she hadn't been able to handle her emotions at witnessing their love.

Abby swiveled her head back in her direction. "I know he does. Some days, I think I don't deserve it. That I don't deserve his forgiveness. But then I remember the sacrifice my brother made, the love Tate shows me, and I tell myself I do deserve it."

"Sacrifice? I don't understand."

Abby glanced away. "Long story." Then she smiled. "You two remind me of me and Tate. He looks at you like you're his entire world, and you look like you think you don't deserve him."

Damn. Bri should've asked her to leave. She was making her dig deep and face emotions she wasn't ready to face.

"He's worried about this case and not solving it. That's all." She stood up and rounded the couch before Abby could see the lie in her eyes. "Want a drink? I could use something stronger than the tea we're having right now."

"I'm game for whatever you have."

Bri walked into the kitchen and opened the fridge, grateful Abby hadn't followed her.

Did Wyatt look at her like she was his entire world? She knew he liked her. He said as much. Plus, his kisses said plenty. But more than like? Possible love? They barely knew each other. All he knew about her was she was a pain in the ass. She didn't know how to let anything go, like her sister's case.

Did it matter what he thought about her? It wouldn't be wise to pursue anything with him because ultimately, it wouldn't last. How could it? They were so different. She worked at a lame diner, and he had a great, meaningful job. He helped people. He put criminals behind bars and gave families peace of mind. Some closure. She served people food.

Closure.

That's all she wanted from Wyatt. Nothing more.

When he came home tonight, she'd be sure to make that clear to him.

STROMBERG OPENED THE DOOR SLOWLY, not sure why. A bit of apprehension, wondering what would happen with Briella tonight, if anything would even happen. He didn't want to pressure her. A bit of annoyance at Abby because although she didn't make Tate mad at him, it was still her fault. If she hadn't come over and bothered Briella, he would've never had to tell Briella—again—not to open the door to anyone. Unfortunately, including his partner, who inadvertently heard that.

Boy, was Tate pissed. He had never endured the silent treatment before. Not even from a woman. Tate played the card well. He barely spoke to him, and only if it pertained to the case.

Sure, he could understand why he was pissed, but he hadn't meant it personally. It was a safeguard for Briella. Make it easier on her. He didn't understand why Tate couldn't see that. So, yeah, he was annoyed at Abby for creating the entire fiasco and he didn't want to see her.

When the door finally swung open all the way, he didn't see a soul anywhere. He also didn't hear a sound. He closed the door, his instincts kicking into gear. Either Briella was already asleep—not that it was too late, only about eight o'clock—or she left.

His heart skipped a beat.

Or *he* got to her.

He could only assume by the silence that Abby had already left. Damn it. Why hadn't he called to tell Briella that he was on his way home? His stomach had been growling for the last hour as he and Tate continued to search for leads in Flora's murder. He didn't expect Briella to wait for him to eat, but he should've called and asked if he should've picked something up.

Hearing her voice would've been nice too. He had missed her all day.

What did the silence mean? He was so damn afraid to find out.

Pulling his gun from its holster, he carefully made his way down the hallway. He wouldn't find any answers acting like a coward by the front door. He could see his bedroom door was wide open, yet the lights were off. As he neared the bathroom door, which happened to be closed, he knew where he'd find Briella. Light spilled out from underneath, a soft, eerie glow coating the carpet.

What would he find?

It was still strangely quiet. If Briella was in the bathroom for some reason, she was too quiet.

Which made him fear the worst.

His hand shook as he reached for the handle.

When he opened it, she screamed, water splashing everywhere as she jerked in the bathtub.

"Wyatt! What the hell!"

He dropped his gaze, even though he wanted to continue to stare. "I'm sorry. I—"

"Get out, you Neanderthal!" Then she threw a sopping wet washcloth at him.

It hit him smack in the chest, plopping to the floor. He made the wise decision to close the door, bringing the wet rag along with him. He wrung it out in the kitchen, then tossed it, along with his clothes, into the hamper in his room.

What an idiot. He could've at least knocked on the door before assuming the worst. Like, that she was dead.

Why would she be *dead*? In the bathroom? The killer always left his victims in the bedroom, laid out on the bed, soaking in their blood, naked.

Time passed. He had no idea how long, but finally he heard a noise from the hallway. He glanced down at himself, realizing he'd been standing in his boxers thinking things he shouldn't. He barely got on a pair of sweatpants before Briella was standing in the doorframe.

"I'm sorry I yelled."

The ache in her tone gutted him.

"Briella, you have nothing to apologize for. I should've knocked. I don't know why I didn't."

Her eyes glossed over his body, roaming from his sorrowful eyes down his chest and only pausing a moment on the bulge that he couldn't control.

"Because you worry too much about me. You shouldn't."

"Good luck with stopping me from doing that."

She smiled, twisting her wet hair into a ponytail, yet didn't put it up in a ponytail or anything. "Did you eat? I wasn't sure what to make, not that I'm much of a cook to begin with."

"No. I forgot about food. I just..." Did he continue to go with honesty? Or should he put on the brakes and leave her alone? Keep his feelings inside?

"What?"

The eagerness in her tone told him she wanted him to keep being honest. But the wariness in her eyes said she was waging a war with herself. That she wanted him to keep his distance as well.

"I wanted to get home to you."

She took a few steps inside, then stopped. "Should we order something?"

He didn't feel like dealing with people, even a delivery person. "How about I pop in a frozen pizza?"

"I'll do it." Her gaze glided across his chest again. "You can get dressed."

Then she twisted around and walked out before he could respond.

It didn't take long to get dressed. He tossed on a shirt and met her in the kitchen where she stood by the stove waiting for it to preheat.

"How was the rest of your day with Abby?"

She shrugged. "Fine. We had one of your beers. Well, two. She had one and I had one. You need better alcohol in this house. I'm not a huge fan of beer."

Okay, at least it wasn't the whiskey and she didn't appear to be drunk. He wanted a levelheaded Briella. There were still some things they needed to talk about. If keeping only beer—ones she barely tolerated—kept her sober, he wouldn't be buying anything else anytime soon.

Then she grinned as she crossed her arms and leaned against the counter. "And you? How was the rest of your day?"

"Fine. Nothing new to report."

Same shit, new victim. It never changed when she asked about her sister's case. It didn't change here either.

"You shouldn't be so hard on yourself."

He decided to mimic her and crossed his arms. "You shouldn't be so hard on yourself either."

"Meaning?"

"You know what I'm talking about. You said last night you killed your sister. You had nothing to do with her death."

"I did. It's my fault."

"Bri—"

"No!" She stood up so fast from her relaxed posture it made him jerk. "You know where I was that night. Picking up my deadbeat boyfriend from work instead of spending the evening with my sister because he insisted his ass needed a ride. On her birthday! We had plans to go out to eat to celebrate a little later than we originally planned because of it. Like a bitch, I canceled on her because I got into a fight with my boyfriend. I thought hounding him about his slutty co-worker and whether they had something going on was more important than being with my sister.

"Then, my selfish ass, thinks it's a good idea to go over to my sister's to cry on her shoulder. He had admitted to liking his co-worker, but he hadn't done anything with her yet. Yet! I was so focused on my own dumb shit, I didn't see how horrible of a sister I was. It was her birthday, but I had to make it all about me! If I hadn't canceled, she'd still be here today!"

A sob tore out of her throat right before she sank to the floor. He was quick to rush to her side, pulling her into his arms, despite her murmured protests. She didn't fight him, so he knew she didn't want him to go away.

"Shhh. It's okay. I know why you feel like it's your fault, but it's not. Whoever killed her would've found another way to do it. Psychotic men like him don't stop because a small obstacle gets in their way."

He wrapped her even tighter into his embrace. The rest of his words that wanted to spill out remained inside. Because he couldn't say that if he'd listened to her last night and left, she'd be dead right now. Which was why she had to stay here, where she'd be safe. Because that same psycho might not stop until he got his way. With Briella dead.

Her tears abated faster than he anticipated. She was pushing on him to release her, at least to the point where she could see his face. He wasn't ready to fully let her go yet.

"You think she was destined to die no matter what?"

Was that what he said? Well, in a roundabout way, he

had. Something he shouldn't have said, not with her in such a fragile state.

"I think you shouldn't blame yourself."

This time when she pushed, her intentions were clear. She wanted away from him. He reluctantly let her go. She stood up from the floor without his offered help and took a few steps away.

"I'm not hungry. I'm tired. Since you made me come here, you can sleep on the couch."

Then she walked out and left him with his heart shattered on the floor.

All he had done today was screw up left and right.

First with his partner.

Now with Briella.

At least the incident with Mr. Becker hadn't gone any further than it should've. No irate call from his captain he'd overstepped, so Mr. Becker was smart enough not to report him. Because it would not have ended well for either of them, and he knew that.

The oven dinged it was done preheating.

Well, he wasn't hungry anymore either.

He slapped the oven button to turn it off and stalked to the desk in his living room where he kept all the cases that kept him up at night. One in particular.

Dawn Colton's.

Briella might hate him, but he'd do everything in his power to find her sister's killer. At least he could offer some peace.

8

BRI TIPTOED CLOSER to Wyatt where he sat with his head resting on his desk, lightly snoring. The obstinate man had been at this desk all night long. A few times she had awoken with a jolt, things she didn't want to dream about going through her head anyway. Each time she had ached to call out to Wyatt. To comfort her. To make the nightmares disappear. Part of her had been surprised he didn't come in at all, if only to check on her.

Well, she had made her point crystal clear last night, and he wasn't dumb in that regard. He had respected her wishes.

As she got closer to him to wake him up, she froze. The pictures splayed across his desk were the last thing she wanted to see.

Her sister frozen in time. Death displayed so sadistically.

She must've made some sort of sound, a short cry of anguish, because Wyatt's head popped up, his eyes blinking, then narrowing his focus on her.

He shuffled the papers until she couldn't see her sister's mangled body any longer.

"Morning." He cleared his throat as he stood up,

glancing at his phone for the time. "Shit. I'm going to be late. How did you sleep?"

His hair was flattened on the side he'd rested on, with the other side standing on end as if he'd been running his hands through his hair way too much last night. Circles coated his eyes, with the tiredness evident even in his slouched posture. Yet, nothing but concern for her well-being sparked through.

"Fine. Your bed is very comfortable." Only part of that was a lie. She'd trade anything for his bed in a heartbeat. Hers sucked in comparison. But being fine? Not even close.

"Good. Ummm...I need to grab a quick shower and go."

"I'll make you something to eat."

"Oh, you don't have to. I normally skip breakfast." He smiled as if what he said would change her mind.

"It's the most important meal of the day, Wyatt." Then she tsked him like he was a naughty child and walked toward the kitchen with a smile.

At least she had removed the concern from his eyes. She didn't like seeing it from him all the time. It might not seem like it to him, but she could take care of herself.

She'd just poured the egg mixture into the pan when he strolled into the kitchen looking refreshed. He'd trimmed his beard and shaved around his goatee. His hair was still wet but styled the way she was used to, combed to the right. He'd put on a white crisp dress shirt with a blue tie and paired it with a black suit jacket. She felt drab in her loose T-shirt and brown drawstring pants compared to him.

"That was a quick shower."

He chuckled. "I refuse to be late. I'd never hear the end of it from Tate." His eyes clouded with sadness, then regret filled the space, his gaze drawing to the pan on the stove.

"You don't have time to wait for me to finish? It's okay."

"You know what? Tate can—"

"You won't be late on my account." She walked to the pantry, looking quickly at everything, then grabbed the last granola bar. "Here. Eat this, at least. You shouldn't skip breakfast."

He took the food without arguing—smart man—then leaned in toward her before jerking back. As if he had been going to kiss her and realized he had no right. They weren't dating. It wasn't as if she'd stayed over because she wanted to. He insisted. He worried about her safety.

Despite all that, she would've taken the kiss.

"I'll, uh, call you later to check in. Remember, don't—"

"Open the door to anyone. Not even Abby or Tate. I got it."

He nodded, hesitated again as if waging a war with himself about the kiss, then left.

Which was for the best.

She finished making eggs and toast, eating most of it. Of course, she'd made too many eggs, thinking Wyatt would be eating too. Wasting food wasn't something she did often, especially on a tight budget most of the time, but saving eggs to eat later sounded gross so she tossed it. It didn't take long to clean up the mess, take a shower, and get dressed for the day.

By nine o'clock, she was bored and chomping at the bit.

She couldn't stay inside all day. Not again.

This killer...

The person who killed her sister...

They wanted her dead now too.

Okay. Not much she could do about that. As Wyatt had said in so many words, her sister would've died no matter what. The killer wouldn't have stopped with a tiny obstacle in his way. Two nights ago, he tried to kill her and found an obstacle. He'd try again. Why wait around for him to make a move?

She was more of a let's-get-it-done-right-away kind of person rather than a wait-and-see.

The killer waited an entire year to kill her. On the anniversary of her sister's death. Since he couldn't have her, he killed an innocent woman instead. Didn't it stand to reason he'd wait until next year to try again with her?

It did.

Wyatt wouldn't agree. There was no doubt in her mind about that. But he also wasn't the boss of her. They weren't dating. Hell, were they even friends? She was the sister of a murder victim. He was the cop assigned to the case. Honestly, she didn't know how to describe their relationship. But bottom line, he couldn't tell her what to do.

She packed her belongings and sent a text before flipping the bottom lock on his door and leaving.

> I know you'll be mad, but I can't hang around your apartment all day again. I'm going stir-crazy. I'll be fine. Stop worrying about me.

Her phone rang before she even got on the elevator. Wyatt, of course. She declined the call. Nothing he said would change her mind. No matter what she said, she knew he wouldn't stop worrying about her either. They both would have to come to terms with that.

She dropped her bag off at her apartment first, cringing at the paint on the wall. Was it paint? It had to be paint. She refused to think of it as anything other than paint.

It didn't matter!

She wasn't about to get a closer look. She'd call a cleaning service to remove it from her walls. Or better yet, management could take care of it. The police had to be done with looking for evidence. If they had found anything, Wyatt would've told her.

Larry, her landlord, said he'd take care of it as soon as possible. He didn't want something like that tainting the building any more than she did. After leaving that mess in his capable hands, she left.

Her phone wouldn't stop ringing with calls from Wyatt, so she eventually shut her phone off.

Was it wrong of her to ignore him? Oh, yeah. She wouldn't deny that. But she wouldn't be swayed by his pleas. If she wanted to walk around New York City for some fresh air, then she would.

Her aimless walking brought her to the cemetery. Not so aimless after all. She usually visited her sister's grave when she felt out of whack. Which, in the past year, had been a lot. Part of her felt like her sister could hear her when she spoke. Not that she ever spoke that much. A few words here and there, then losing her voice when the tortured emotions crawled up her throat, stopping her.

She slumped to the ground, resting on her knees.

"I don't know what I'm doing, Dawn. I can only hide from Wyatt for so long. He'll find me and..." She sighed. "Make me come back to his place. Or insist he stay at mine. And for what?!"

She leaned her head back, staring at the bright blue sky, the sun shining down as if its brightness could spark a bit of joy in her.

"The same guy who killed you wanted to kill me. He killed some random woman instead." She swiped a tear away as she drew her gaze back to her sister's headstone. "Another death on my hands. Another person dying because of me. I'm so sorry, Dawn. I know I say it all the time, but I'm so sorry for what I did to you. Now I need to apologize to this other woman."

Bri laid her hand on the grass as if she could feel her sister get closer to her. "I could use some advice with Wyatt. I don't know what to do about him. He makes me feel...well, I guess, he just makes me feel. Other guys were nothing compared to how I feel about Wyatt. What's worse is I would've never met him without losing you. I hate that. I don't deserve that or him or anything good when you're not here. Help me, Dawn. Help me find the right path to take. You were always telling me what to do. To do better in life. I always ignored you, told you to mind your own business. Well, I'm listening now. Tell me what to do."

Of course, nobody answered. Nothing happened. No sounds. No signs. No indication that her sister's spirit even lingered. This was why she rarely spoke to her sister. Nothing ever answered in return.

So Bri did what she always did when the grief consumed her.

She cried.

He sat rigid in the seat, staring straight ahead, trying to figure out where to look for Briella next. When he raced home to his apartment, she had been gone. She'd cleaned up all traces of herself as if she'd never been there in the first place. His next stop had been her apartment. A crew hired by the landlord was erasing evidence that cruelty had ever stepped inside her place. But no Briella.

Throughout his entire search, Tate stood by his side—in silence. The bastard was still pissed off at him. At least, he hadn't abandoned him altogether.

This was all his fault. He massively screwed up this morning.

"I should've eaten the eggs. I didn't eat the damn eggs."

The first audible sound erupted from Tate along with a heavy sigh. "Why are you rambling about eggs?"

"She offered to make me breakfast this morning and I didn't want to be late. I would've been late if I stayed. I told her don't bother. She did anyway. The eggs were cooking and I left."

"She did not leave because you didn't eat any eggs."

Stromberg punched the dashboard, his fist ringing with pain, though he didn't care.

"Hey..." Tate said calmly as if he were a riled horse waiting to spring into action. "I'm not saying you did anything wrong either. I'm just saying this has nothing to do with eggs."

"Yeah." His gaze swiveled in Tate's direction, the urge to punch his face strong. "Then what is it about?"

Tate's expression mirrored his own. Taut and ready for anything. "Nothing to do with you. I guarantee it. The anniversary of her sister's death just passed. Some psycho wants to hurt her as well. It's a lot for anyone to deal with. You gotta...shake it loose."

Stromberg stared at him, hating his own words thrown at him.

Wow.

They were more annoying than he realized. By the shit-eating grin Tate wore, he'd done it on purpose. To irate him. To get under his skin.

To make him feel something other than panic. Did that mean Tate wasn't pissed at him any longer?

Tate swore under his breath, then ran a ragged hand down his face. "I get it, man. I know how you feel. Every horrible piece of pain sitting in your gut. You want to protect her from everything. You can't, no matter how hard you try. I'm sorry."

Well, that was new. They'd said some pretty nasty stuff to each other over the past few months, especially when they first met. They didn't make it a habit of apologizing to each other.

"For what?"

"For getting pissed about telling Briella not to answer the door for me. I get it now."

One problem solved. Tate wasn't pissed at him anymore. He'd take it. To show his thanks, he wouldn't utter the words shake it loose ever again. Maybe.

His shoulders slumped as he leaned back into his seat, defeat taking over.

Honestly, he'd take an angry Tate over Briella missing.

"Where to next, partner?"

He tossed his hands in the air. "No damn clue. As much as I'd like to say I know Briella, I don't. I don't have the faintest idea where to look for her. She's off of work for a week, so I doubt she'd go there. There's nothing I can do until she returns my calls."

There was a moment of silence. As if Tate didn't want to say out loud, "if she returns them at all." Because that's what went through Stromberg's head.

"Let's go back to that bar. Yesterday they said Nick would be in today. I'd like to talk to him."

Tate nodded and pulled away from the curb. No more beating the Briella topic to death. There was nothing left to say. She left this morning, and he had no idea where to find her until she wanted to be found.

They made it to Gunner's Bar in a decent amount of time. Traffic wasn't too bad, and Tate always had a lead foot when driving. Stromberg usually drove, but when Briella sent him that text, he must've looked like he lost his mind because Tate nabbed the keys before he could.

The interior was dark, a faint musty smell permeating the air when they stepped inside. Two dingy lightbulbs were lit, but not enough to see everything clearly. The place probably hadn't been cleaned in ages. Most likely why they didn't brighten anything up. Stromberg didn't even want to know how many health code violations the place had. Not his concern at the moment, or ever. He'd never have a drink or eat here.

A dude behind the bar was playing on his phone, leaning against the back counter. He looked up with disinterest. His clothes were clean and his hair smooth with not a strand out of place. The longer he stared at them approaching the bar, the more a dangerous glint flared to life in his eyes. It said he'd get down and dirty and mess you up with one wrong word.

"You must be the detectives who were looking for me yesterday. I don't know how I can help you concerning Flora."

Meaning Nick didn't *want* to help them.

"Detective Powell," Tate said, then pointed at him, "Detective Stromberg. We have a few questions. We'll start with how many times you sexually assaulted Flora."

Nick flared to life, bouncing to the other counter that separated them. Muscles ticked in his jaw, his biceps flexing. Putting on a show, as if that would deter them from further questioning. Not likely. While he wouldn't have started so in-your-face as Tate had, it got the job done. Or maybe he would've. He could feel the rage bubbling up inside again—like it had with Mr. Becker.

"I never touched her any way she didn't want it."

Tate leaned against the bar, not displaying an ounce of fear that he'd put himself closer to Nick. "Not even once? Not a tiny slap on the ass? Not a rub on the cheek? Last time I checked, doing shit like that without a woman wanting it is sexual assault, no matter how small of a touch it is."

"Where are you getting your information from?" Nick snarled, as if that would sway them in any way. Stromberg was waiting for Tate to unleash holy hell on this asshat. If not, he'd be more than happy to do so.

"Where were you two nights ago?" But Tate also knew his limits. It was one thing to piss off someone, it was another to risk his badge by laying hands on said person. Stromberg was past the point where he didn't care. He'd do anything to find his killer.

"Working."

"Well, Tony, your supervisor we talked to yesterday, said you weren't here. Would you like to try again?" Stromberg jumped in, though with a lot more venom in his tone than Tate.

"My other job," Nick growled through his teeth.

"And that would be where?" Why did some suspects— and oh, he'd been added to the list the moment he opened his mouth in Stromberg's eyes—have to make things so difficult for no reason?

"Bouncer at Flaming Flamingos. Got there at eight and didn't leave until three in the morning. There's always a huge-ass line. I was in front of people all night long."

"Even on your break?" Tate added.

"I don't take breaks. Now if that's all, get the hell out."

"Did you have any problems with Flora?" *Besides the unwanted touching.* Stromberg left that out because it felt implied.

"Flora was a flirt. She liked to tease, and I teased right

back. Nothing ever happened between us though. It's one thing to tease, it's another thing to dally with one of the waitresses. Tony doesn't like that kind of shit, and I don't ever get on the wrong side of Tony."

Stromberg had to admit that sounded like the first honest thing Nick had imparted thus far. At least the Tony part. He didn't believe for one second Flora flirted with this douchebag. He'd been the first one to even suggest she was a flirt. No one else they had interviewed described her in that way.

"If you think of anything that would be helpful, here's my card." Stromberg laid his card on the bar and walked away. No doubt he'd throw it away the second they walked out. If he didn't walk away now, he knew he'd put his hands on another suspect, roughing him up more than he did to Mr. Becker.

"Damn," Tate said, slamming his door. "I wish I could say he's our guy, but it doesn't feel right. He's a sexist jerk, but not our killer."

He hated how his gut said the same thing.

"Agreed. Which brings us back to square one. With jack shit."

He pulled out his phone, dialing Briella again. Voicemail once more.

Temptation pulled on him to punch another fist into the dashboard. He found himself squeezing the phone instead to stop the impulse.

"Why don't I call Abby to reach out to Briella? Maybe she'll have better luck."

At this point, he'd try anything.

"Do it. Then let's get this killer before anything happens to her."

9

HER JEANS HAD GOTTEN dirty from sitting on the ground at her sister's gravesite. She didn't even care. What was a bit of dirt and grass stains when her sister couldn't even breathe anymore?

Though it had hit mid-afternoon, she needed caffeine. Lots and lots of caffeine. Her mind was frazzled, and her body felt like she'd been in a war and lost. That's how much she had cried. At least no one had been around to witness her weakness.

She sat in the back corner of the cafe, sipping her mocha latte and munching on a brownie. Not much of a lunch, but it was something. She'd turned her phone back on but continued to ignore Wyatt's calls and texts. The man was determined. Why did she expect anything different?

"Wow. Briella, long time, no see."

She flinched at the voice, then her eyes widened when she saw who stood in front of her.

"Bryan Lauder. You're right. It's been a long time."

If one considered a year a long time. The last time she had seen him was at her sister's funeral. He and Dawn had been good friends since childhood. Dawn had considered him one of her best friends.

She stood up and hugged him, albeit awkwardly. While she knew him well enough, she hadn't been besties with him as Dawn had. She had her group of friends, and Dawn had had hers. Bri's friends had always run more along the lines of rowdy and ridiculous, while Dawn's had been laid-back and, quite frankly, boring, in her opinion.

She sat back down, gesturing at the chair on the other side of the table. "Would you like to sit?"

"Just for a few minutes." He pulled out the chair, taking a sip of his drink. Probably straight black like the dull individual he was. Judgmental and harsh of her, sure, but the truth was the truth.

"How have you been? I haven't seen you in this neck of the woods in...a long time."

Again, he meant since her sister's funeral.

Generally, when she visited her sister's grave, she went back home, which wasn't anywhere near this place. Today, she had felt like a coffee. This place wasn't too far from the cemetery.

"Good. I have good days and bad days when I think of Dawn. Overall, life is fine."

She didn't see the need to go into the whole ordeal of someone wanting to kill her. Way to bring a conversation down.

"And you?"

He nodded. "Same. Can't complain too much. You look good."

And he was a superb liar.

She knew she looked terrible. Her eyes looked like a raccoon—not to mention red from her recent crying bout—and her hair was thrown into the messiest ponytail she'd had in a while. Not to mention she wasn't wearing any makeup. Good thing too, since she had balled her eyes out.

Despite his outright fib, she smiled in thanks. "You do too."

His sincere grin in return didn't calm her senses. If anything, they ratcheted up a notch. This had been the most awkward situation she'd been in recently. Working at a diner, dealing with different people all the time, awkward was the name of the game. She couldn't pinpoint why she felt so out of place in his presence. But she did and she didn't like the feeling.

"Anyone special in your life?"

She nearly spit out the drink she had taken but managed to suppress her surprise. Why did he want to know? It wasn't as if they had these kinds of conversations when her sister had been alive. More like simple pleasantries and she went on her way. When Dawn's friends had been around, she'd been scarce. Because again— boring!

Did one consider Wyatt special? If so, then yes, she did.

"Kind of. It's a complicated relationship." Close to the truth. She had no reason to lie to him. "And you? Any lucky lady?"

He smiled behind his cup before taking a sip, making it appear mischievous in a way. "I'd have to say the same. It's complicated."

Well, that was an interesting answer. Especially for someone boring like him.

Her phone took that opportunity to ring. If it had been Wyatt, she would've answered just to get Bryan to leave. But it was Abby, and she would also work to solve this situation as well.

"I'm sorry, I have to get this. It was nice seeing you."

He took the cue for what it was and stood up. "You too. Until we see each other again."

Then he walked away.

Odd choice of words. She had no desire to see him again.

"Hey, Abby, how's it going?" She hadn't expected to hear from Abby so soon, even though they had exchanged numbers yesterday. Or maybe this shouldn't be a surprise. "Or should I be asking how Wyatt is?"

"Stromy is worried about you. I can report you're a-okay, right?"

Now that Bryan was out of her atmosphere, yeah.

"Of course, I need some space."

"Oh, I get that. Totally. But look, here's the deal with men like Stromy. He's an alpha. He's not going to stop and he's never going to change. He's going to worry like an infection that doesn't go away. He's going to care about you like no man ever has. I only know this because he's like the exact replica of Tate."

Interesting way to describe him, but Bri could see all of that being true.

"So what are you telling me?"

"That pushing him away is only hurting both of you." Abby paused. "Unless you don't like him. Which I highly doubt."

No, Abby was correct in her assessment. She liked Wyatt. She had for a long time. She couldn't even pinpoint when he'd gone from a detective working her sister's case to a man she desired.

"I can't stay holed up in his apartment forever. Or until he catches this guy. It's been a year, he still has no leads. What does he expect me to do, move in and never leave? Because at this rate, this killer will never be found."

"I wouldn't suggest that idea to him unless you mean it because he'll insist you move in. He wants to protect you. They can't help themselves. Tate's the same way."

"Well, I'm not moving in with him." They weren't at that level in their relationship. If they even got that far.

"I know that. I get not wanting to be stuck in one place. But there is also some sicko out there that wanted to kill you a few days ago. It's a little early to be running around the city alone. At least give it a week before you put yourself in danger."

Bri wanted to snort at that. A week? Was that a sufficient amount of time before putting oneself in danger? According to Abby, it was. She wasn't sure she agreed.

"A fixed target is still a target. So is a moving one."

Abby huffed. "Are you saying you're trying to draw this killer out?"

"I'm not a wait-and-see kind of girl. I thought Wyatt knew that about me."

"I'm sure he does. But I don't think he foresaw this coming. If you want to be bait, fine, I'm not against that. But having backup isn't wrong either. Where are you?"

This was happening whether she liked it or not. Having people back in her life who cared. She'd managed to push everyone else out of her life since her sister died. Now, people wanted back in. New people. Ones she knew she could trust with her life.

"Are you going to tell Wyatt where I am?"

"No." There was another moment of silence. "By the end of the day, you will. Because I know you know it's the right thing to do. You can't ignore him forever."

Her intention when she left this morning hadn't been to ignore him forever. She felt the walls closing in and needed to leave.

She rattled off the location and ended the call. Her coffee was almost empty, so she ordered another one with a cookie this time and got comfortable in her seat.

Then sent another text.

> Abby's meeting me. I get why you sicced her on me. I'm not mad. We'll talk later tonight so stop blowing up my phone.

"Well? Are you going to tell me who texted you and what it says? Because staring at your phone like that is starting to annoy me."

Stromberg shook his head, as if that would shake the turbulent thoughts out of it as well. *Shake it loose.* Yeah, that expression was starting to wear thin. It didn't work. The worry consuming him since this morning when Briella had left still held permanent residence.

He held up his phone so Tate could read it. He didn't want to say it out loud. It wasn't horrible what she wrote. She wasn't mad. There was that. But he didn't like how she said they'd talk later tonight. He had a feeling he wouldn't like what she had to say.

"There you go. Problem solved. Abby to the rescue."

The shit-eating grin on Tate's face had him clenching his fist as if he'd actually punch the asshole. Oh, and he wanted to so badly.

Tate's gaze drew down to his fist. "If you plan on using that, I will do more than give you the silent treatment. I'll dump your ass as a partner. You know it was the right call. Abby is the best person to help her through her shit. Abby's been through more than Bri has."

Honestly, it was getting damn near close to them being through the same amount of shit, but Stromberg wasn't going to argue semantics with him.

"You're a jackass."

"And you're an asshole," Tate shot back.

Stromberg relaxed his fist, remorse hitting him. "I would never hit you, even as tempted as I am sometimes. I hate admitting you're right about Abby. I have a bad feeling I won't like the chat with Briella tonight."

Tate relaxed his stance as well. "I had a few tough conversations with Abby when all that shit went down with her brother. It has to happen, no matter how much we want to avoid it. Bottom line, what are you looking for here? What do you want from her?"

All of her. Her thoughts, her feelings, her trust. Because the way she left this morning suggested she didn't trust him at all to keep her safe. He'd already thwarted the killer once. Unintentionally, but still. It counted.

"I can tell you I don't want her walking away from me. I don't want to just be the damn detective working her sister's case."

"Well, then stop beating around the bush about it. Tell her." Tate took a step closer, his expression fierce and unyielding. "You tell her how's it going to be. And you don't accept anything less."

He frowned. "I'm sensing you did the same with Abby."

Tate nodded, retreating as he'd gotten his point across by getting in his face.

Stromberg shook his head, laughing. "And how did that work out for you?"

Tate cocked a brow. "It could've gone better. So that's why you need to do better than I did. Stay strong and in her face and tell her how it's going to be."

Yeah, he foresaw himself failing as much as Tate had with Abby.

Tate tossed his head toward the club they'd left after verifying Nick's alibi. "Let's go before they come out and wonder why we're still hanging around."

They left, walking to the vehicle with Tate driving. They chatted with a few more neighbors of Flora's, friends, and people around the neighborhood. Nothing new arose. Same dead-end they had yesterday and the day before that.

He hated how eerily similar it was to Dawn's case. No leads, no suspects, no evidence.

The autopsy had been performed. Raped and beaten, then stabbed to death. The killer hadn't been kind in any aspect of the attack. No defense wounds, suggesting he got the upper hand right away and was strong throughout it. He hated thinking about how much she suffered until she died. No matter how much he told himself not to, he couldn't help it. Her face would morph with Dawn's, and sometimes, Briella's even popped into his head. Her body the one beaten and bruised. Dead in a pool of her blood.

"Hey!" Tate yelled, snapping him out of his tormented thoughts. "Are you going to be okay tonight? Do you want Abby and I to come over as well? Maybe having a strong force in front of her will help her see how serious this is?"

Stromberg had no doubt she understood the seriousness of it all.

She simply didn't want to be caged in. She didn't want him calling the shots. That could mean only one thing.

She didn't trust him to do his job. And why should she? He hadn't done a damn thing to solve her sister's case. What made him think he'd solve Flora's?

"No, it's okay. I need to do this on my own."

Tate nodded. "Call me if you need me."

Tate went his way, and Stromberg went his own. He thought about calling Briella before showing up but didn't. She wouldn't have picked up his call anyway.

While he didn't know if she was at her apartment since she hadn't told him where she was yet, he concluded that's where she'd go at the end of the day.

He hesitated before knocking on her door.

It opened less than a minute later, and he was surprised how fast she came to the door. For a moment, he thought she'd ignore him. Keep him out and away from her as long as she could.

She looked tired and worn out. He looked the same way. He knew the feeling.

She nodded her head for him to enter and walked to the living room, taking a seat on her small brown couch that had seen better days. He closed the door, locked it, then took his shoes off before taking a seat next to her. Keeping his distance wouldn't close the gap between them. A gap that had enlarged to an impossible distance since this morning before he left.

He managed a glance at the wall, grateful to see the blood had been removed. A slight stain marred the wall, but he figured the landlord would have it painted in no time.

"What did you and Abby do today?" He figured he'd start with polite conversation. Because he knew before he left—no doubt she'd kick him out—they'd be having more than just polite words. It'd get very volatile in here soon.

"Had some coffee, did some shopping. We even thought about getting our nails done, but I hate gels and regular nail polish comes off right away. It's annoying."

Not what he expected to hear, but it sounded like a normal day. Honestly, he wasn't sure what he had expected them to do together. Certainly not look for a killer on their own. Tate would have Abby's hide if she did something dangerous like that.

"And you? What did you and Tate do all day?"

She asked it so innocently, as if he hadn't heard the sarcasm laced in each word.

"Worked Flora's case with the hope we'd find something and nothing. A very disappointing day." In more ways than just the case he couldn't solve.

She looked away. Maybe because she hadn't expected him to answer so truthfully. Maybe because she had and still hated the answer.

"Are we going to talk about it? Why you left?"

There was no time like the present to get the difficult conversation out of the way. Why delay the inevitable? It wouldn't change the outcome.

"No."

He narrowed his eyes. She would not be getting out of this that easily.

A smirk appeared on her lips. "You need to tell me something first."

Well, as long as she labeled it as *first* this conversation and then his, he was more than willing to cooperate.

"Fine. What's that?"

"Why don't you like your first name? You never told me yet."

He frowned. It was a long story and he hated hashing it over. People always called him Stromberg and he rarely had to acknowledge his first name.

"It's a lovely name. I don't get it. I want to understand."

But if it got her to talk about why she left, then so be it.

"It's my uncle's name. I was named after him. He and my father were very close as kids. My dad was younger than him and always looked up to him. They had a close relationship. I did too with my uncle." His mind floated back to the horrible memories. "Until we didn't."

"And?" She giggled, more so he figured to reduce the tension filling the space between them than anything actually being funny. "What happened?"

"Well, my uncle decided to have an affair with my mother. My father found out, of course. Because he wasn't a dumb man. It hadn't gone on long before he found out. They had words..." He hated thinking about that time in his life. "Then it turned into a fight." He sighed. "And my uncle killed my father. He's now sitting in prison with life without parole."

Briella's mouth dropped open, not expecting that bombshell. Most people didn't, not that he shared the story often. Never, in fact. But on rare occasions, his secret emerged, and he had to nip the situation in the bud.

"It was a pretty open-and-shut case. I was thirteen when it happened. The detective that showed up...well, I'll never forget his kindness. His compassion. Even for my mom, who I blame for part of it."

If she hadn't slept with his uncle, the fight would've never happened. His relationship with her had been strained the rest of his teenage years. When he turned eighteen, he moved out and never spoke to her again. She knew it would be a losing battle trying to gain his forgiveness, so she never attempted contact in return.

"That's why you became a cop. Isn't it?"

He nodded. "My father was the victim in all of it. It made it easier to live without him knowing justice was served to my uncle. From that day on, I never wanted to be called Wyatt again. I hate the reminder of him. Of what he did."

Then he reached forward, touching her thigh. "For the first time, in a long time, I don't cringe when you say my name. You don't have to stop calling me Wyatt. I like hearing you say it. It erases part of the horror that I remember."

She frowned. "How? How could you want me to keep calling you Wyatt? What you went through...I lost my sister. Why did you never tell me you lost your father in the same way?"

"It wasn't in the same way. It was cut and dry with my dad. He beat my dad so badly, he killed him. My uncle was still there when the police showed up. I called them myself. I hid in my room through it all, but I called them. I didn't say anything because I don't talk about it. I don't tell anyone about my past or about why I don't like my first name. People just know not to call me Wyatt."

He squeezed her thigh to get his point across. "I won't stop you from doing what you want to do. You can call me Wyatt. Like I said, I don't mind it from you. It helps the hurt I feel. I don't know why. I can't explain it other than there's something special about you."

"I'm sorry for your loss."

It had been a long time now since he lost his father. He'd had years to get over it. Some days, it hit him hard and he could hardly function. Those were the days he threw himself even more into his work. To forget the pain. So he understood loss. He understood the pain she went through. He understood what all of his victims' families and friends he helped find justice for went through.

"Evil lives everywhere. Sometimes, we don't even know how close it is to us." He leaned closer, and for some odd reason, she averted her gaze when he did so. "Which is why I worry like hell about you. Why did you leave today?"

Time to get back on track and to the topic he wanted to have the most.

She snapped her gaze his way, her eyes slicing him to the

bone. Just like that, her irritation and anger were back. "I won't be holed up with nothing to do. And for how long? How long do I stay cooped up waiting for you to find this killer?"

Another year were the unspoken words he heard. He couldn't blame her. It was a good question.

When he didn't answer her—couldn't really—she smirked, nodding.

"Yeah, that's what I thought. You're never going to find him."

Ouch.

That hurt.

The lack of faith in him. But he couldn't dispute it, no matter how much it gutted him to the core. He'd had a full year to find her sister's killer, and instead of doing his job, he let the killer strike again.

Her expression fell into despair the longer they stared at each other. He had no good rebuttal, so he didn't say anything at all. He couldn't say anything that would make anything better between them.

"Wyatt..." She leaned closer, placing a hand on his chest. She hadn't shoved his hand off her thigh, so he considered that a good thing in addition to her touch. "I shouldn't have said that. I know you're trying to find this killer. Telling me about your dad and what happened, I have a much better understanding of you. Why aren't you saying anything?"

He removed his hand from her thigh and placed it over hers, as if that would keep her close to him. "Because I have nothing to dispute. Everything you say is true. I've failed you. I failed Flora. I don't know what to say other than..."

Tate said to put it all out there. Confess his feelings. Didn't she already know how he felt? He kissed her. He showed her he wanted more. Why put more of his heart on the line when he knew nothing would work out between them? It seemed cruel to dangle his heart in front of her. Such wishful thinking.

"Other than?" Her brows pleated as the pressure on his chest increased. "Tell me. You wanted this conversation, so don't hold back."

Don't hold back? She didn't know what she was asking of him. But okay. She'd get the full unaltered truth from him. She'd already gotten more from him than he'd ever shared with any other woman. He'd never relayed the story of his father before to a girlfriend.

"You could've told me before I left you weren't going to hang around. Instead, you send a text and make me worry out of my mind. I can't tell you what to do. I know that. I have no right, but I'd like to be in this together. I'd like to fight this unknown entity together." He wrapped his free hand around her neck, pulling her closer. "I want to be together. In every way that you can think of. I need you in my life more than I can express. So losing you in any way—and that includes you walking away—guts me to my very soul."

And he did it anyway. Let his heart have hope that she'd reciprocate his feelings.

He heard a slight hitch in her breath, obviously surprised by his candid words. Well, she had asked for it.

"You won't like what I have to say."

He didn't doubt that. He knew it even before he arrived.

"Say it anyway."

Her hand on his chest fisted his shirt, her nails scratching him. She had a death grip on him now. Same as he had on her with his hand around her neck. It would take a lot of force for him to let go. Though neither seemed to be headed in that direction.

She let out a deep breath. "We know he wanted to...kill me. Flora was collateral damage. You say you failed her. Well, so did I. That should've been me, not her."

Heaven help him, but he couldn't be sorry that Flora died instead. Losing Briella was unimaginable. He'd never utter those words to a soul, but his mind would know the truth.

"We know he's not going to give up. What we don't know is if he's going to wait another year. I can't live my life in fear. Not for a whole year. Not for a month. Not for a week. Not even for an hour. I won't, Wyatt. Do you hear me? I will not live in fear."

His fear was ratcheting up by what she was saying. He didn't like the direction it was going.

"You're getting to the part I won't like. I can sense it."

A wisp of a smile graced her lips. He wanted to kiss her instead of finishing this conversation.

"If I stay in a place he can't find me, it doesn't end. The fear wins. If I continue my life as normal, he has a way to take another shot at me."

The pressure on her neck increased so much she winced, moaning. The last thing he wanted to do was hurt her, so he let go before he did something worse. He even removed his hand holding hers that was on his chest. Though she didn't release her death grip on him.

"Absolutely not. You're not making yourself bait for this asshole."

"If not me, then who? Who will die next? Another woman who wasn't meant to. It's not like I'm doing anything special to grab his attention. I plan to live my life like I always do. I will not let him win. I will not let him control me." She pulled him closer, her eyes narrowing. "I will not let you control me either. You have no say in what I choose to do."

He grabbed her by the shoulders, hesitating, wanting to push her away. "I *want* a say in what you do. That's what I'm trying to tell you. I want to be in your life more than just a damn detective!"

"Then we compromise. I get a say in what you do." She released his shirt, bringing her hand to his cheek, caressing it. "You're not the only one with feelings here. I don't know when it happened, but it did. I fell for you. I found myself going to the precinct, not to badger you about my sister, but to see you. To feel something for a brief moment in time. Because every other minute of my day is spent feeling nothing. Nothing but regret and despair and so much hatred at myself that it's hard to get through the day. When I'm with you, I feel something better. I feel tiny moments of happiness. Like my life can move on."

Wow.

Holy hell.

That moment of hope he'd given his heart a little bit ago wasn't for nothing. He had to be dreaming. Conjuring words he thought he'd never hear.

"What do you want me to do?" He wasn't sure how to respond to everything she said, his own emotions embattled in a war he couldn't describe. So he picked the one thing that would be easier to digest.

"I want you to support me in my decisions."

"That's not a compromise. That's giving you what you want. What about what I want?"

"You want me to stay hidden in your apartment away from the world. That's not going to happen."

"No, I want you to be safe. Did I like you in my home? Hell, yes. The selfish part of me loved it. Any reason will do to have you in my domain. But I would never make you do something you don't want to do. You want your own surroundings. Fine. You want to live your life. I can't argue with that. My compromise then is you let me stay over. You don't go off alone anywhere. Live your life, but wisely."

She dropped her hand from his cheek, and he felt like he'd made a misstep somewhere. The loss of contact was a dagger to his heart. He dropped his own hands from her shoulders waiting for the ultimate blow. Where she demanded he get out and never come back. She asked for a compromise, he was trying to give her one.

"You're not trying to dissuade me from anything."

His brows dipped, trying to decipher her question. Or was it a statement?

"I know enough about you to know when to pick my battles. With what was slapped across your wall,"—he pointed at the now clean wall devoid of any message—"I could argue with my captain about protective custody. That your life is in danger. I chose to bring you to my apartment instead for safety. I ignored the proper way to do things. I broke protocol and pretty much put my badge on the line bringing you to my place. This killer threatened you. You're right, will he wait a whole year? We have no idea. You asked for a compromise, I'm giving you one. I want to be by your side whenever possible. I want you to never be alone. I want you to live your life, but with it never leaving your head that there is a killer out to get you."

"No, Wyatt—"

"I will not—"

She grabbed the front of his shirt again, this time pulling him until their mouths met. She crushed her lips to his, and he could do nothing but go along for the ride. He'd soak up every morsel she was willing to give him. He didn't know if he'd get it again.

The kiss ended as abruptly as she started it.

"You didn't let me finish, you fool!" She shook his shirt, her nails grazing his skin. "I was going to say, no, Wyatt, you're not understanding me. I'm shocked you're compromising with me. You're not trying to talk me out of anything."

"I will if it comes to a point that I think you're being reckless."

"Why would you think I'd ever be reckless?"

His mind ventured back to the whiskey bottle and her cutting her hand. Oh, she could be reckless without warning. She knew it too but wanted to feign innocence. He'd ignore the question altogether.

"So it's settled. I'm spending the night." He paused for a beat. "In your bed. With you."

Her brow rose steadily as a crafty smile emerged. "With or without clothes? I mean, since we're negotiating right now."

He matched her smile with his own sly one. "Without, since you're asking."

Her hand loosened, then brushed a path down until it settled on his lap. Her smile died. "I am scared, you know. All the time. I don't know how to get rid of that. Now this... him making such a statement. It scares me. I don't want to let it consume me."

He cupped her cheeks. "We're in this together. From here on out. I won't let anything happen to you. Do you trust me?"

"With all my heart."

God, he didn't know how much he had needed to hear that.

"Then trust me when I say I will never stop until I get this bastard."

If it was the last thing he ever did, he'd lay down his life for her.

How dare she! Who did she think she was?!

First, she let that damn detective stay over on a very special day. And now she was letting him back in.

He figured since she left the detective's apartment this morning and removed his little message off the wall, she had seen the light. She had used that minuscule brain of hers to realize that he meant business.

She was off-limits to everyone!

Except for him.

Why couldn't anyone ever learn when he told them something? It was just like at work with all the imbeciles he had to endure every day.

Like Dawn when he confessed his love. She'd laughed and rejected him. She had thought he'd been kidding.

He did not kid around. Not with something this important. His feelings mattered. What he wanted mattered!

Well, she'd learn her lesson—again. It would stick this time.

They were meant to be together. As soon as she understood that, he could explain everything. He could tell her how sorry he was that he killed her sister. It had been an accident.

He wouldn't apologize for Flora. That had been a consequence of her bad behavior.

Now, he had to be cruel once again.

He had to punish her for her defiance.

10

AFTER MAKING a quick meal of ham sandwiches with chips, they snuggled on the couch and watched TV. Bri didn't even process much happening on the screen. Having Wyatt's arm around her, feeling his warm heat, his strong presence captured her attention. It had been a long day, and she didn't have the energy to focus on much.

Not even his heartbreaking story about his father and uncle. To think they shared a common bond on losing someone so horribly.

Of course, she had never had the inkling Wyatt would cheat on a woman. He was too kind and considerate for something so callous. Now she knew he never would. There was no doubt in her mind. Not after what his uncle and mother had done. It had completely ruined his childhood. It had made him hate his first name.

She trusted him. In all the ways a person could trust someone. So if he said he didn't mind her using his first name, that it helped heal part of the hurt inside, then she'd continue to call him by that name. Calling him Stromberg felt weird. She thought Wyatt was the sexiest name ever.

Having to call him Stromberg like everyone else didn't feel right.

Not more than an hour passed before he suggested they go to bed. Probably due to the fact she had dozed off on him. So she agreed without complaint.

He ran to his car for the overnight bag he kept in his vehicle for emergency purposes. She chose to believe that, instead of him coming prepared that she wouldn't kick him out. She changed into her PJs, brushed her teeth, and snuggled underneath the bedcovers by the time he came back inside. It didn't take him long to get ready for bed and slide in next to her. Before he did, he took a chair from the dining room and shoved it underneath the bedroom door after also locking it.

She stared at the door as she rested her head on his bare chest.

"I know this is a silly question to ask, but I'm doing it anyway. Why is there a chair underneath the handle?"

Wyatt tensed, then covered his hand with hers that had been drawing a path up and down his chest. "You told me management changed the locks to your apartment, which is good. But this guy is getting into places, and I don't like not knowing how. He's skilled at breaking and entering. The last time I was here with you, I didn't even hear anything going on out there. I'm generally a light sleeper. An extra barrier of protection doesn't hurt."

Of course, that all made sense. Which was why she knew it had been a silly question. But still.

"You didn't do that at your apartment."

"I also didn't sleep in the same room as you. I was the barrier between the front door and where you slept."

She lifted her head, frowning. "I don't want you getting hurt because of me, Wyatt."

He swiped a tender hand across her cheek, smiling despite the tension swirling around them. "I would die for you."

"Don't say that. Don't ever say that."

"Why?"

The crease between her brows increased. Why? He was going to ask her why? Because! She shouldn't have to explain why.

His hand brushed her cheek again and she hated how much she loved his soft touches. Getting used to being in Wyatt's arms wasn't wise. She could see herself falling in love with him, and then where would that leave her? With a broken heart, because she messed up every single relationship she ever had. Even the one with her sister, and they were bonded by blood.

"I'm not just here to protect you, Briella. I'm here because I want to be. I know things are crazy right now, and not the best time to start a relationship, but that's where I'm headed with you. I will do what I have to to keep you safe. Because if something would happen to you, I'd never forgive myself."

"Likewise, Wyatt. I don't think I could move on if that happened."

"You had no problem with me sleeping in another room last night. Now I put it into words you don't like, and it changes the narrative. It wasn't a big deal. Why are you making it into one?"

She sighed, then rolled onto her back, staring at the ceiling. He was right. She was making this more than it should be. It was only smart to keep another barrier between them, in case this psycho decided to try something else.

They'd had a long, honest talk earlier, and while she was

glad they had, it was still hard to let someone in. Every time she did, her life went to shit.

And if she was being honest with herself, seeing him put a chair underneath the door made the threat even more real. That's what scared her the most.

She had even told him she wouldn't live in fear. So what did she call this? The fear was taking control and ruining what could be something beautiful between them.

Twisting back his way, her hand brushed his beard, loving the roughness but knowing he was soft and sweet on the inside.

"I'm acting like an idiot. I'm sorry."

He moved some of her hair out of her face and behind her ear. "You're not an idiot. I get it. And it's okay. You never have to hide how you're feeling with me."

"In the past year, I haven't been with anyone. Dating wasn't even a speck on my radar."

He nodded as if he agreed that he hadn't wanted to date anyone either, but he didn't verbally agree.

"I don't have any condoms in the house." Her hand slid down his chest until she hit his boxers, then it dipped underneath, grabbing ahold of his cock that was hard and ready for action.

He sucked in a harsh breath, jerking at her touch. "My bag has one."

She giggled. "Why does your emergency bag contain a condom?"

"For moments like this."

Her hand stroked up and down, relishing in the way his breathing went from light to heavy, his hips moving with her ministrations.

"And how often do moments like this occur?"

His hand wound around her neck, bringing her closer.

"This would be the first time. It will remain the only time. I will always be prepared for you."

Then his lips were on hers, his tongue diving in, the heat around them rising in intensity. The kiss turned fierce as her hand increased in its pleasure. Tiny groans of delight slipped from Wyatt's lips, turning her on even more.

"Ok, stop," Wyatt said breathlessly, pushing her away. She was forced to let him go. "Condom, now. I'm not coming without you."

He jumped off the bed before she could protest, not that she wanted to. Her panties and tank top disappeared and so did his boxers before he joined her once again. The condom went on quickly, and then he was on top of her.

His brows pleated as his hand dipped to her center. "I'll make you feel good first."

She could tell by his expression he had a hard time waiting, but her needs superseded his own. She'd never doubt how he felt again. Only a good man worried about something like that. While she enjoyed how he touched her, wringing her emotions out with ease, she didn't want it to happen this way.

She pulled his hand away. "Together. We do this together or we don't do it at all."

The tightness in his face decreased and a smile lit up his lips. That's right. They were in every single thing together.

He positioned himself, then slid inside her. She'd been waiting for this moment a long time, even if she had tried pretending to herself she didn't want this to happen. The anticipation of it had her so wet, he had no trouble. They both sighed with glee when he was all the way in.

He bent down, kissing her neck. "Damn, you feel even better than I imagined. I'm going to have a hard time holding back."

She wrapped her legs around him, pushing him even deeper. "I don't want you to hold anything back."

He took that as his cue. He lifted slightly and pumped his hips with no restraint. In and out he pounded into her, and she enjoyed the moment for what it was. Something new and more than she could express.

Sure, she'd had more sex than she cared to admit. It wasn't something she was shy about. But it was just sex.

This?

With Wyatt.

She felt more connected to another person than she had before.

The fact he wasn't holding back made it that much sweeter.

The sensations flowing through her body made her ache for more. More of everything that he could give her.

"Harder, Wyatt. I need you."

He gripped her thighs, pounding as deep as he could. "How's that?"

His wicked grin said he'd do anything for her as long as she continued to tell him.

She bit her bottom lip, returning a sly smirk of her own. "A little more." A sultry moan escaped when he thrusted even harder. "Yes, Wyatt!"

She knew her cries urged him on because he forged on with his quest to love her body as thoroughly as possible. The bliss spreading through her body was coming to an end, she could feel it.

"So close," she whispered.

He rocked two more times before the euphoria hit her, calling out his name with a throaty breath. He kept thrusting before his orgasm hit, tensing and growling in pleasure.

His body went slack and rested on top of her, then light kisses hit her neck and cheek. "I knew it would be like this with you. I knew we'd be dynamite together."

"And how did you know this?"

Because she had wondered a few times if they'd even mesh well together. Of course her wariness of letting others in always held her back.

"I can't explain it. I knew that if this ever happened, it'd be something I'd never want to give up." His expression turned fierce, his eyes glowing with possession. "I won't give you up, Briella. You're mine now."

She'd dated a few possessive assholes in her life. None of them ever lasted long because she didn't do well with being told what to do.

But when Wyatt said it...

It felt more like a reminder that she wasn't alone anymore. That he was there to help her fight whatever obstacle jumped in her path. That he'd defeat the monsters in her head that tried to stop her from living the life she deserved.

His lips brushed against hers. "Did you hear me, Briella? Say it. I want to hear you say it so I know you understand what I'm telling you."

He'd always been bossy, since the first time she spoke to him right after she found out her sister had been killed.

And she knew he'd never change.

"You're mine now."

His mouth curved into a devious smile when she repeated his words, though not exactly as he had demanded. He wanted her to say I'm yours. She knew that.

But now he knew the same applied to him.

"Good."

Then his lips sealed the deal with a searing kiss that told

her round two was about to happen. Too bad they had no more condoms left. They'd simply have to get creative with their pleasure.

"Well, the shit-eating grin says you got lucky last night," Tate said with a wily smirk as they sat across from each other at their desks in the precinct.

He had walked inside the building with a pep in his step. Even when he sat down, the grin hadn't disappeared. Nothing they had to do today was worth smiling about.

"Which is interesting when I thought she was pissed at you."

"We made up."

Tate chuckled. "And then some."

"Whatever." Stromberg rolled his eyes. He wasn't about to kiss and tell. Tate never did, and frankly, he didn't want to hear any sordid details about him and Abby.

The conversation ended—thankfully—and they got down to business. The day dragged on with no leads to tackle. Unfortunately, Flora wasn't their only case, so they had to set her aside and work on some other ones. That's what happened. When a case went cold, you moved on. Unless something small popped up, there wasn't anything they could do at the moment.

Not that Stromberg intended to let it sit for long. He swore he'd find this killer and that's what he planned to do.

Throughout the day, he texted with Briella. He didn't like knowing she was home all by herself, but seeing as he knew she wasn't about to budge in any way, he had to go along with it.

Some of the texts even turned hot and heavy. Which

made him go hard, creating uncomfortable situations at times. Having an erection while talking to potential witnesses wasn't very professional. Yet, he couldn't stop himself from flirting back with her. She'd even sent one text with her breasts on display, tweaking her nipple. He nearly told Tate then and there he had to leave. He didn't feel so well. Except he caught himself before he did something so reckless. When he got to Briella's place tonight it would make their joining that much sweeter.

By the time he got off work and made it to her apartment, he was so damn horny he didn't think they'd even make it to the bedroom.

He knocked on her door harder than he intended. When she didn't respond right away, he knocked again. By the third time, his heart raced with too many horrible implications.

Something was wrong.

It doused his libido like an icy shower dumped over his head.

"Briella!" This time he pounded where the whole damn hallway could hear him. "Briella!"

He pulled out his phone, dialing her number. It rang and rang until the voicemail came on.

"No, this isn't happening," he muttered under his breath as he tried calling again.

He needed a key to her apartment. Why hadn't he gotten a key to her apartment? If he had to kick down the door, he would. There would be no hesitation.

She still didn't pick up.

"Briella!"

Pound. Pound. Pound.

"Briella! Open the door!"

He was about to slam his foot against the door when it

finally swung open. His heart rate didn't lessen a fraction, even seeing her beautiful face.

Her eyes were red-rimmed as if she'd been crying. They were also glossy. The whiskey bottle dangling in her hand confirmed why.

He pushed her to the side, slamming the door. Despite his anger, he managed to lock it so he didn't forget.

"You're home!" She giggled then tried to wrap her arms around him, but he held out his hands, keeping her away.

Giggles? When he knew she'd been crying. There was no way in hell he was about to let her ignore whatever might've happened.

"What happened?"

Damn it! He meant to have the conversation about the whiskey bottle as well. Now look what happened.

"What makes you think something happened?"

It was like a damn roller coaster with this woman. Up and down, going around crazy insane curves. He never knew what was coming next. Would it be a sharp turn? A nosedive? A dark tunnel with no escape?

"Why are you drinking?" He snatched the bottle out of her hands, causing her to cry out.

In pain? Because he wasn't gentle when he grabbed it. But he figured more from the loss of it than anything else.

"Give that back."

"You're done turning to the bottle when you can't handle something." He stormed to the kitchen and started pouring out the golden liquid into the sink.

"No!" Briella tried to shove him away and yank the bottle from his hands.

Of course, he was stronger than her and had a decent grip on the bottle. He barely moved and neither did the bottle.

"Stop it, Wyatt! I need that!"

None of her cries impeded his goal. Not even when she called him a bastard and a few other unsavory names. Not even when she cried in agony that he was dead to her.

She didn't mean it. It was the liquor talking.

Even if it wasn't, he had told her last night that she was his. *Mine!* And nothing, not even some damaging words, would change that fact.

When the last drop emptied, he dropped the bottle into the sink, it clattering to its side.

"Now," he said with strained patience, "tell me what the hell happened to make you cry and go for that bottle."

Her anger had seemed to dissipate, and now the sorrow was returning. Her eyes filled with water as her bottom lip wobbled.

What had gone wrong in the last two hours? They hadn't texted in that timeframe. Before that, she had sent the sexual picture telling him she was eagerly waiting for him to get home. So, in less than two hours, something made her get drunk to the point she couldn't even stand without wavering on her feet. He was ready and waiting to grab ahold of her if she lost her balance.

Silence filled the space between them. He didn't continue demanding anything as he knew whatever it was would come out sooner or later. He wouldn't have it any other way.

A few tears slid down her cheeks.

He stepped closer and brushed them away. "Talk to me, Briella. You scared ten years off my life when you didn't answer the door right away."

She stumbled as she turned, pushing his hand away when he tried to help her. He followed her into the living room where she picked up her phone from the couch and threw it at him.

"That happened."

Their texting?

He didn't understand.

It had been a mutual conversation. She'd engaged with him as if she wanted to. Hell, she had sent the naked picture!

He tried to unlock her phone but didn't know her passcode.

"I can't get in it. What am I supposed to look at? I thought what we—"

She knocked her leg into the coffee table when she tried to reach for the phone, crying in pain. She shoved him off again when he attempted to help her. The phone disappeared from his hand, her fingers punching angrily at the screen. Then she tossed it back at him. He nearly dropped it, fumbling with it before getting a decent grip.

The text she'd opened had his stomach dropping to the ground. He hit play on the video.

Flora screamed as someone held her down, pleading for her life. Another scream erupted when a knife punctured her skin. The video went on for another five seconds of more of that horror before stopping. The text below the video said, "This is your fault."

Now everything made sense. The crying. Grabbing the bottle and getting piss-ass drunk.

Her quiet tears had turned into sobs. He set the phone down and drew her into his arms, grateful she didn't push him away once again. He guided her to sit down and from there pulled her into his lap as she let it all out.

He squeezed her so tightly, he swore he'd find bruises on her arms later. But he didn't care. He needed her to feel that she was safe. Nothing could harm her. Not the madman playing cruel games with her.

"That is not your fault. He chose to kill her. You had nothing to do with it."

Her sobs increased, but it didn't stop him from consoling her and repeating over and over that it wasn't her fault.

Though he wanted to know, he didn't ask why she didn't call him right away when she received the text. It sent her into a tailspin and all rational thought had fled. It didn't matter in the long run. Flora was dead, and they had no leads.

Unless he'd be able to extract something from the video. Despite the disgust filling him up, he knew he'd have to watch the video again.

And again.

And again, until he found a new path to follow.

11

———

STROMBERG STOOD in the kitchen near Tate as he watched the video. Stromberg chose not to watch it. He'd already watched it several times before Tate and Abby arrived. It had taken Briella a long time to calm down. Once she had, he told her he had to call Tate. She'd nodded then excused herself to the bathroom. Her steps had been wobbly, but knowing she needed a moment to herself, he didn't follow.

He'd made coffee while it sounded like she took a shower. By the time she got out, he had a mug waiting for her—as strong as he could make it—and Tate and Abby had arrived. She was now silent on the couch while Abby sat next to her quiet as well, but there for her if she needed her.

"Damn," Tate muttered under his breath, then he looked at him. "Is she okay?"

Since there was a solid wall between them, he couldn't see her, but he had to guess no. When they walked away toward the kitchen, Briella had her shoulders hunched, her face crestfallen. That wasn't someone who was okay. Though she was sipping the coffee he made and sobering up. Once the effects of the alcohol wore off, he might get more than just tears out of her.

"She's hanging in there. Hell, I'm not even okay. That bastard not only brutally raped and killed that woman, he taped it!"

He exhaled a large breath, chastising himself for raising his voice. Neither woman stormed into the kitchen at his outburst, which shouldn't have surprised him. Briella was still locked in her own world. Abby wasn't going to leave her alone.

Tate hit play again, and all Stromberg could do was try to drown out the screams. When the video stopped again, Tate sighed.

"There's not much here to garner from the video. He wore gloves. He had a steady hand while he stabbed her. Can't even distinguish his race because no part of his skin is revealed."

Stromberg nodded, agreeing with the assessment. After the fifth time watching the video while Briella had been in the shower, he had stopped, knowing it was useless.

"I don't get why he's taunting Briella now. Why wait a year? Why kill again on the exact anniversary of her sister's death?" He blew out a strangled breath. "When is he going to try and hurt Briella? That's the question that kills me the most."

Tate clamped a hand to his shoulder, gripping hard. "We will not let anything happen to her. As soon as we find this asshole, he's going to regret it."

Stromberg feared he'd regret it more than anyone else. He worried that he would fail her. That this bastard would find a way to kill her and there wasn't anything he could do about it.

Tate's hand slipped away, and then he repeated the video again.

Stromberg turned away, cringing at the screams. "How many times are you going to play that damn thing? I thought we already decided there wasn't anything to decipher in it."

The sounds stopped. Tate sighed.

"I know, but I can't help myself. We're missing something. Why'd he send it in the first place?"

"To get under her skin. To show her he has all the control and power. To tell her he can get to her at any time."

The phone hit the counter with force, clinking loudly. "Like hell we'll let him. Maybe we've been looking at this case all wrong. From the beginning, you focused on Dawn. The people she knew, the places she went. The people who had a problem with her. It made sense, she was the victim."

Stromberg twisted back around, frowning, waiting for Tate to get to the point.

"Maybe it's always been about Briella. We need to start looking at the people she knows. At the places she goes. The people who have a problem with her."

"You think Dawn was an unintended victim?"

Tate shrugged. "I'm sensing it's someone they both know. Flora was collateral damage. She doesn't factor into anything. He came here a few days ago for Briella and ran into an obstacle. You. So he took it out on the first person he came across. Flora. Grabbed her off the streets so it wasn't hard to get inside her apartment as she was with him.

"Now, Dawn's and Briella's apartments, those are different stories. How did he get in? Sure, a master at breaking and entering is possible. I won't discredit it. But he also could know them both and made a key. Someone they trusted. Someone who could've made a copy without them being wiser. You didn't hear anything a few days ago. How did he get in? How did he throw that message on her wall without you hearing anything?"

Tate picked up the phone. "This is personal. This isn't someone suddenly fixating on Briella. He has patience. He's been watching her a long time. I guarantee it. Maybe he thought the kill would be sweeter to wait for the anniversary of her sister's death. Now he's frustrated. He's going to start losing his patience."

He hated everything Tate was saying, yet he couldn't disagree with anything either. It made sense. Too much sense.

The part where he was losing his patience, nothing good would come from that.

"Now what do we do? Briella is not exactly going to cooperate. I know it." Stromberg ran a hand down his haggard face. "She refuses to cower in fear. While I get that, I hate relinquishing control. She won't listen to me. I tried. I gave in because I'd rather have her by my side than a door slammed in my face."

"Abby can be the same way." Tate's lips thinned though his eyes shimmered with glee. "Sometimes, you have to do what you have to do to lay down the law."

Stromberg snorted, shaking his head. "Yeah, because that worked so well for you. Abby didn't listen to a damn thing you said, and you know it."

Tate rolled his eyes. "Okay, so she can be stubborn. So can I. Look, this video changes things. Bri has to understand that. She was a robot when we got here. She's in shock. It'll wear off, and then she'll listen to what you say."

Stromberg doubted that. She might follow directions in the beginning, but she'd change her mind again. Like she had the first time.

"Let's get her phone records. We'll try to trace where this text came from." Tate gripped the phone again. "I doubt we'll get anything good, but it's our next step."

"I can't leave her."

Tate nodded. "I know. I'll take care of it. Abby can stay if you want."

It was whatever Briella wanted. Whatever made her feel better, safer.

"It doesn't matter."

Nothing did except keeping Briella safe and out of the hands of a killer.

———

SHE PULLED her legs up onto the couch, wrapping her arms around her knees. She barely acknowledged Abby or Tate as they left. What was there to say? She was a fool. They knew it. She knew it.

Even Wyatt knew it.

Silence filled the space between them as he took a seat next to her after locking the door behind the other two.

Her head fell to her propped-up knees and her gaze met his.

"Say it."

He frowned. His eyes said he wanted to reach out to her, but his body was shifted away as if preparing to run because he knew this wasn't going to be a pleasant conversation.

"What do you want me to say?"

The shower and the two cups of coffee she consumed had helped to diminish the copious amount of whiskey she had pilfered, but alcohol still swam through her senses. She wasn't that drunk that she was talking nonsense. He knew what she was demanding of him.

"You know."

The tense lines filling his forehead increased, then he shifted back, resting against the couch cushion.

"I don't know what you're waiting for me to say."

Her head straightened. "I'm an idiot."

"How so?"

Seriously? He wanted her to spell it out for him? How cruel could he be?

Before she could retaliate with something she'd regret saying, his hand drew closer, brushing against her cheek.

"I get it." His hand went back to his side. "None of us expected that video. To think he..." Wyatt swallowed hard, shaking his head. "I know what you saw was...horrible. But don't think for one second that any of it is your fault. I'm not even sure why you think you're an idiot in this situation."

Well, she didn't understand either. It was the only sensation that coursed through her veins since her mind had returned from the alcohol-induced vacation.

She should run to the liquor store and get some more. Go back to the numbness. Where nothing could hurt her. Bother her.

"Why would he send that to me? Why would he record..." She hiccuped, the tears gathering in her eyes and the sobs bubbling in her throat.

"He's trying to scare you. He's—"

"Well, it's working!"

The sobs won, ripping out of her as if a demon had torn her soul right out of her body. Wyatt gathered her into his arms, holding her, rubbing her back. He said nothing, but she didn't need pointless words right now. She needed to know she was safe. That he was real and here and nothing could harm her.

Somehow, she found her way from the cushion to his lap, his warm arms wrapped securely around her. The tears eventually subsided. In their place came a headache. Partly due to the alcohol mixed with the crying.

"What's next?" she whispered, hating to ask. It couldn't be anything good.

"Tate's going to try to trace where the text originated from."

"I doubt this person is that dumb."

Wyatt sighed, gripping her tighter. "I know, but it doesn't hurt to double-check."

"Are you mad at me?" She sat up when she asked it, needing to see the truth in his eyes. Not that she suspected Wyatt would lie to her, but just in case. It was always easier to see the truth in a person's eyes than through their lips.

"I have no reason to be mad at you."

"That wasn't a no."

His gaze tore away from her for a brief moment, then back, the pain bleeding through. "You didn't call me right away. You received that disgusting text and instead of letting me know about it, you decided downing an entire bottle of whiskey was a better idea. I'm not mad at you about that, but I'm hurt. I'm confused and I'm hurt. If you don't trust me to—"

"No, Wyatt," she cut in, bringing a hand to his roughened cheek, "it had nothing to do with trust. I panicked. Horrible scenarios entered my head and terrified me. My sister's body punctured my mind. The thought he has a video of that too...I couldn't take it. I wanted to erase it all. For a brief moment in time, when the whiskey took control, I didn't think about it. My mind wouldn't let me. I wish I could have that feeling back right now."

His hand found her neck, pulling her closer. "You don't need whiskey to drown the pain. That is not going to solve anything. I need you to start turning to me instead. Let me take those images away."

Then his lips were on hers, dragging her body as close to his as possible. She sank into his embrace, running her hands through his hair. This method would work too. She didn't mind Wyatt consuming her instead of the whiskey.

His hand possessed her neck, his other one pressed deeply into her back. Even if she wanted to get away from him, she wouldn't be able to. He had her locked in his arms. Exactly right where she wanted to be.

The kiss he bestowed upon her was thorough and filled with all the erratic emotions she'd felt throughout the day. The anticipation of him coming home. The thrill of teasing him. The shock of the video. The passion overriding any other senses.

"Briella, we..."

His words drifted away as she wouldn't allow him to stop what was happening. He wanted her to come to him instead of turning to the bottle, then he would give her what she wanted.

She grabbed the hem of his shirt, yanking it up. Their lips broke apart while she stared at the obstinate article of clothing.

"Get this off you now. I will rip the buttons if I have to."

His eyes dilated with pleasure, the moment of apprehension he'd experienced moments ago gone.

"Then you better get your clothes off as well. I need to see you. Touch you. Do all the things my mind conjured throughout the day."

She stood up, de-robing nearly as fast as he did. Then

she was sliding back onto his naked lap, running her hands through his hair once again. She sighed at the same time he did.

Then their lips connected once again as his warm hands scaled up her back, then down again, tracing tiny sensual circles around her hips.

"I can't hold back much longer," he murmured against her lips, his hands trailing to her thighs.

"Let's stop waiting and messing around." She found his cock, hard and ready for her, then guided him to her, sitting down as the sensations drowned out any evil that threatened to enter.

"Oh, Briella," he moaned, his head falling back against the couch as his hands tightened around her thighs.

She took that as her cue to ride him as deep and hard as she wanted. He encouraged her, his hands sliding to her ass, gripping and pulling her deeper. The pleasure, the need inside her consumed her. She wanted more. She wanted him so deep, she'd feel the effects into next week.

Her low moans mingled with his deep growls. Everything about him drove her wild, made her feel free and like nothing could go wrong.

"So close. Keep going, baby," he murmured breathlessly as he sat up, latching onto a nipple. His teeth suckled, then nipped, grazing the skin. Painful for a moment, then soothing and erotic in the next.

Her hands wrapped around his head, urging him to suck harder. Bite harder.

She needed the pain. She needed the ache only he could smother with his sharp yet delicate touch.

Then it happened. She tipped over the edge as his teeth sank in. She cried out his name, holding his head there, his lips devouring her nipple until the ecstasy coursing through her veins was too much.

She let Wyatt lean back as he continued moving her up and down to reach his own pinnacle.

"I'm so damn close. I'll tell you when to get off."

Her fingers slid through his hair, grabbing the ends. "No. I'll stay right where I am. Come for me, Wyatt. Let go."

His lips twisted in pain, his eyes searching for any sign of misunderstanding. "Maybe you forgot, but I didn't get a chance to slide a condom on. What we're risking right now—"

She bent down, her lips brushing his. "I'm on the pill. And even if something would happen, I'm prepared to face those consequences." Her lips swept across his again. "Are you?"

His eyes blazed with desire. More than she had anticipated. "We're never using a condom again."

Then he pumped his hips with a vengeance, gripping her ass as he plunged inside her so deeply, she knew it wouldn't be long until he fell over the edge.

And then he did.

He grunted, exhaling, then pulled her closer, squeezing her so strongly she nearly couldn't breathe.

"Briella..." he whispered in her ear, brushing a hand against the back of her head. "I expect more erotic texts tomorrow. Because this sex was off the charts."

She giggled, having no issue with that request whatsoever. She'd enjoyed the day, teasing and torturing them both.

Then the other terrible events of the day came crashing in. She trembled, and he instinctively knew it wasn't in a good way.

"We'll catch this bastard."

He grasped her face, demanding she look at him. His hands were like a hot poker on her cheeks, searing her to the bone.

"I love you. Nothing and no one will ever hurt you again."

12

THE CHAOTIC NOISE of the diner was a welcoming sound. Odd how she'd missed this. Johnny in the kitchen screeching for people to get their asses moving when he was the slowest cook on the planet. Beth chewing and snapping her gum behind the counter as she helped the regulars who came in every day. Even the craggily old busybody who sat in the corner was a blessing.

Since receiving the disturbing video, the rest of her week consisted of her sitting on edge, waiting for Wyatt to get home, and having the most amazing sex to drown out the horror. Then doing the same thing the next day. No matter how many times she tried to remember if she knew Flora from somewhere, she couldn't say she did. Why pick her to murder? What did she do wrong? And why send Briella that disgusting video? What did this madman want? To her irritation, she couldn't answer any of those questions.

She was happy to be at work. Something new to change up her routine. She'd been staying at Wyatt's apartment, conceding that his building had better security. In less than a week, she'd moved in with him. It's the fastest she'd ever moved with a man and yet, it felt right. Like she'd been waiting her whole life for someone like him. Someone who made her world feel like it wasn't teetering on the edge of madness. Though, she didn't technically move in, move in. She still had the lease on her apartment, not that she'd been there often lately. Pick up things here and there, but that was it.

After saying hello to all her coworkers, donning on her black apron, she fell into the easy routine of waitressing. Life was good. Life was starting to feel normal once again. Though she didn't go anywhere alone. Wyatt dropped her off at work and picked her up. Their evenings were spent together or with Abby and Tate. If she needed to go to a store, she went with Wyatt or Abby. She made sure she was with people at all times. Some nights, Wyatt had to work late. Abby came over. Problem solved.

For a month, this was their routine. They fell into it so fluidly. It didn't bother her in the least. Wyatt made her feel safe and secure, like nothing could hurt her. The only time she hesitated about what they were doing was when her rent had been due. She paid it, despite not having slept in it since that horrifying day she received the text. Officially moving in with Wyatt seemed like a big deal. They hadn't talked about it, and she wasn't ready to have that conversation. At least, not yet.

Bri found herself jumping when Beth stopped next to her, popping her gum.

"What's got you on edge?"

Nothing. Not at the moment, anyway. She didn't like someone sneaking up on her. That should've been obvious to Beth, especially with the things she'd been dealing with lately.

"You know I hate it when you pop your gum in my ear."

She rolled her eyes, though the smile on her face said she wasn't saying it in a rude way. She did despise it though.

"Sorry." Beth returned a smile and then snapped her gum again. She couldn't help it, and Bri had given up telling her to knock it off.

For a Tuesday, it was slower than usual. Midafternoon, they normally had more stragglers than what occupied the space currently. Bri wasn't going to complain. She'd woken up today with a slight headache and a crick in her back. The slower, the better.

"So, how's it going with you and that hottie detective? Why does he always drop you off and pick you up? Possessive or something?"

Or something. Some might see it as possessiveness, and Beth clearly did if she asked. But Wyatt was doing what he could to keep her safe. No other gross videos or texts had been sent to her, but that didn't mean the killer wasn't lurking.

"The faster I get home, the faster we can have sex."

Beth snorted, then her brows rose when Bri didn't giggle like she was kidding. "Oh, you're being serious."

Half serious, anyway. They typically had sex as soon as they got home. They liked to tease each other mercifully during the day with naughty texts.

And it wasn't as if she was going to go into detail that it wasn't safe for her to take public transportation by herself. Flora had been swiped right off the street. No one the wiser. She wasn't taking that chance. Neither was Wyatt.

"The subway takes too long."

Beth busted out laughing, slapping the counter. "Only you would find someone hot as hell and makes you come every single damn day."

She couldn't hold back the smug grin. "It's a first for me. I'm enjoying it."

No other boyfriend had ever been as attentive in the bed as Wyatt. Hell, they didn't always even use a bed. They'd marked up his entire apartment, from the kitchen to the living room, the shower, and even the hallway.

"He got any hot friends?"

There were a few other handsome detectives he worked with. Tate was ruggedly handsome, though utterly devoted to Abby. Rider had a nice smile and decent manners. A few other guys she'd met in the past month more intimately since dating Wyatt.

None that she'd send Beth's way though. The gum chewing alone would send them running in the opposite direction.

She shrugged. "Yeah, a few. I don't know them that well."

Which wasn't a complete lie. But again, none she liked for Beth.

The bell above the door chimed. Steven, a regular most days except the weekends, strolled in, taking his usual spot at the counter.

Beth popped another bubble, grinning. "I guess I'm up." Then she grabbed the coffee pot, pouring Steven a cup because he always started with two cups of coffee before ordering his meal.

Two more hours and she could chill with Wyatt. She didn't feel like cooking. They normally took turns making supper, which put tonight as her turn. Maybe he wouldn't mind ordering pizza. The thought of standing at the kitchen counter, preparing something had her back tingling with more pain.

She didn't know why it hurt so much today. She had

tossed and turned a bit last night too. She must've tweaked it sleeping somehow.

Her phone buzzed in her pocket. A smile spread across her lips when she read it.

> Feeling like ordering pizza tonight. What do you think?

Did Wyatt know how to read her mind? Purely coincidence? Somehow, she doubted that. The man was so in tune with her emotions, it was kind of scary sometimes. Like now.

I love you. Nothing and no one will ever hurt you again.

Those words drifted through her mind every single day. He'd said those three little words over a month ago, and though he had yet to repeat it, she knew he loved her. He just didn't want to make her uncomfortable. Considering she had not reciprocated.

She didn't know how she felt. She'd never fallen in love before. This fast? Could you fall in love that fast? But was it considered fast when they'd known each other for a year, even though they hadn't dated the entire time?

All she knew was she cared deeply for him and couldn't imagine him not in her life. Perhaps that meant she loved him. But she wasn't ready to say the words yet.

> I was thinking the same thing. Stop reading my mind. Lol

> So don't tell you that I plan to give you a nice, long back rub tonight?

She bit her bottom lip, grinning so ridiculously she didn't care what anyone thought of her. Of course he noticed her back had been bothering her this morning.

Oh, no, please do go on with what else you plan to do tonight.

She loved these moments. The teasing. The build-up. Then eventually coming together with so much passion she was surprised they hadn't gotten any noise complaints against them.

Her lips swept downward the instant the next text came through.

Not from Wyatt.

Her fingers trembled so much, the phone slipped from her hand, smacking the ground hard.

Beth threw her a look. "Girl, you okay?"

When she met Beth's gaze, Beth pushed away from the counter and stalked to her, picking up her phone as if she knew Bri couldn't pick it up herself. Beth's skin turned pasty white as she stared at the screen. "What the hell is this shit?"

She had no words. That whiskey bottle she hadn't touched in the longest time was calling her name. Where was Wyatt when she needed him?

"Sit your ass down before you fall over." Beth pushed her to the end of the counter and around to the other side, shoving her onto a stool. Then Beth fiddled with Bri's phone.

"Yeah, this Wyatt? You might want to get to the diner right now. Some sicko just sent a text to Bri."

She drowned out the rest of the conversation, her mind running wild. She hadn't even hit the video to see who'd be on it. All she knew was it wouldn't be pleasant.

"He's on his way. What do you need?"

She needed her life to go back to what it used to be. For her sister to be here and none of this ever happened.

That would mean Wyatt never entered her life. Right now, she'd take that over this madness.

HE BARELY LIFTED HIS HEAD, not wanting to give away he watched her as she fell apart reading his text. No need to draw attention to himself. Not that anyone would notice him anyway. They never did.

Her back was to him, so he couldn't see if she was crying or not. He hoped so. She deserved all the tears for the torture she was putting him through. Defiling herself with that detective. Ignoring him! Pretending like he didn't exist. He didn't ask for much from her. A little recognition. A little caring toward him.

Except nothing.

No gratitude for the things he did for her. Moving in with that detective! Ignoring him! He would not abide by it.

Well, she'd show a little respect now. She'd finally understand he wasn't playing games anymore.

His message should be received loud and clear.

And if not...

He'd keep sending them until she understood. Keep making her wait and wonder when he would strike next.

STROMBERG WHIPPED OPEN THE DOOR, the bell above it jangling with too much force. He spotted Briella at the counter and stalked to her in four long strides.

"What happened?" He didn't wait for her to answer, pulling her into his chest. She didn't resist, burying her head as a shiver rippled through her.

"Here." Beth stood on the other side of the counter, pushing Briella's phone closer to him. "I'd keep the volume low. I couldn't even watch the whole thing." She turned her face away for a moment. "Why would someone send her something like that?"

Damn it. Not again.

"That's what I'm trying to figure out. Her shift is over."

Beth nodded, her eyes narrowing as if he'd said the most outrageous thing and should be ashamed. She grabbed something from underneath the counter, then plopped Briella's bag onto it. "I talked to Ron. She can have the next few days off."

Stromberg didn't know Beth well. Hell, he didn't know any of Briella's friends well. He hadn't met any of them. While he said hello to some of her co-workers in passing when he picked her up after her shift, he didn't stick around to chat. But he decided he liked Beth. She was a good friend.

"Thank you."

He swiped Briella's phone off the counter along with her purse, then guided Briella to stand and follow him outside to his car. He'd watch the video without prying eyes and ears around. He got her situated in the backseat, then rounded the car and slid behind the wheel. Tate was silent in the passenger seat, glancing at Briella but not saying a word. Her head was hanging low, her arms wrapped around her body.

Her phone felt like a hot poker in his hand. Tate glanced at the device, then at him. Neither said anything. Neither made a move to look at the text either. Since the moment he received the call from Beth, racing to the diner as fast as he could, they hadn't said one word. What was there to say? The bastard was at it again. Why? What was his endgame?

"Watch it already," Briella whispered, her head still hanging low.

He and Tate shared a look before he opened her phone and hit play on the video. It was similar to the last disgusting video he'd sent. Only this time...

It was an unknown victim.

He'd killed again. They hadn't been notified yet.

Every second was as disturbing as the last one had been. The screams. The terror in her eyes. The way he laughed as she fought for her life. The revulsion as he whispered right before it ended, "You're welcome, Briella."

What the hell did that mean?

Why would she thank him for something like this?

Tate blew out a breath, the first real sound to hit the confines of the car.

"There's not much to tell based on the angle of the video. Where they are. Until we get a call..." Tate rubbed a hand down his face. "Seeing who sent the text will be another dead end like last time."

Stromberg nodded, agreeing with everything.

"I know who it is."

They both twisted toward Briella.

He tapped the screen. "You recognize her?"

She gave a tight nod and finally met his gaze. "She lives in my apartment building. On the first floor. We've chatted a time or two. She even came to the diner last week for lunch. I wouldn't call us friends though. She did make a complaint against me a few months ago for being too loud. My apartment is right above hers. I apologized because I *was* loud that day. I had a bad day and I needed music to drown out the...noise."

Maybe that's why he said you're welcome. Because they

had an issue in the past and he thought the woman had been a problem for Briella. So, he eliminated the problem.

"Drop me off at home, Wyatt. I know you're going to have a long night."

He didn't want to leave her alone. Not for one second. She seemed to be taking this video much better. Or was she putting on a show so she could break down when he wasn't there? The hell with that! He wanted to be there for her in every kind of way. Especially the difficult times.

She leaned forward before he could rebuke what she said, brushing a hand across his cheek. "I'm going to be fine. I refuse to let this asshole control how I react. He wants me to fall apart. I won't let him do that to me. So, I need you to figure out who this is and stop him. You can only do that if you work the case."

He drew closer to her, wrapping his hand around her neck. "I am so sorry he's doing this to you. You are so damn strong." Then his lips brushed hers and, despite knowing she was afraid of hearing it, he whispered, "I love you."

She trembled and closed her eyes but didn't back away. He took that as a good sign. When she didn't return the sentiment over a month ago when he first said it, he thought he'd ruined everything between them. Except they'd only grown closer since then. He had decided until this entire case was closed, it was better to keep those words inside. He didn't want to give her any reason to leave him. Pushing her away—scaring her away—was the last thing he wanted.

But he needed her to know right now that her bravery was one of the reasons he loved her so much. He'd never met anyone as courageous as her.

"I don't want you alone."

Her eyes popped open. "Maybe Abby wouldn't mind coming over."

"She's on her way there now," Tate interjected, causing them to pull away and relax back into their respective seats.

Briella offered a tiny smile. "There. Nothing to worry about then. Abby and I always have a nice time together."

That didn't mean he wouldn't worry about her every second he was away from her.

Stromberg settled into his seat and started the vehicle. He dropped Briella off first, holding her close and kissing her as if he'd never see her again before leaving her with Abby.

They arrived at Briella's apartment and asked for the building manager to open Kelly's apartment, stating they were doing a wellness check. Though they knew what they'd find behind the door.

They found her in the bedroom, blood soaking the mattress and floor.

"Why is he doing this? Why send that video to Briella? We searched and dissected her life a few weeks ago and found nothing. He's picked her for a reason, and we can't find the damn reason why!" Stromberg slammed his hand to the wall, nearly putting a hole in it. His hand and arm vibrated from the hit, and he wanted to do it again, despite the pain making its way into his body.

Tate grabbed his shoulder, as if sensing what he wanted to do, and squeezed. "We'll look again. We'll find who is doing this. We won't stop until we do."

When she received the first nasty video, they did a deep dive into her life. The people she knew. The men she had dated. Anyone she'd had a problem with in the past. Everyone they interviewed had been cleared. They had an alibi for the night Dawn and Flora had been murdered. But apparently, they'd missed a few things.

He hadn't known about the incident—despite how small it had been—between her and her downstairs neighbor. Insignificant, but clearly something now. Whoever had killed Kelly had known she'd filed a complaint against Briella. How? Where did they find their information from? Why kill her over something so dumb? Briella had even apologized, and life went on without any other problems between them.

"Come on. Let's call this in. We don't want to mess with the scene until we're given the all clear."

Stromberg agreed only because he knew they wouldn't find anything useful. They had yet to do so in the first two crime scenes.

He followed Tate out of the room and into the hallway where they called for reinforcements. Stromberg sent Briella a text, unable to stop adding three little words to the end of it.

> We found her. I'm so sorry. I'll be home as soon as I can. I love you.

Her response was short and portrayed she was doing fine with Abby. No profession of love, not that Stromberg had expected one. Hoped for, sure. But he had an uphill battle when it came to getting her to admit she loved him in return.

It would be one battle he'd actually win. He wouldn't lose her from his life. She was his, and she'd have to accept it.

After waiting for the coroner, who estimated a time of death between six o'clock to twelve o'clock last night, they left. Of course, not before interviewing a few neighbors who were home who hadn't heard or seen anything suspicious.

They were planning to interview Kelly's boyfriend—kindly informed she had one by her next-door neighbor—when his captain called. His words had been short and clipped. "My office. Now."

When they arrived at the precinct, Tate followed him in the room, assuming their captain meant both of them. Nope.

"Sit," Captain Wilson ordered with a sharp point of his finger to the chair in front of his desk as soon as Tate walked out and closed the door.

Stromberg didn't argue. He had a strong, scary inkling why he'd been called in here.

"Well?"

It didn't mean he would confess anything when his captain demanded in one simple word to do so. Maybe it wasn't for the reason he was thinking. If that were the case, he couldn't risk letting his secret out.

So, he stared at his captain, waiting for him to elaborate.

"I heard Briella Colton received another text from this killer. You found the body already."

"Yes, sir."

His captain sighed, resting back in his chair as if all the fight in him had died. As if he'd exerted all his energy in his short, clipped responses and he had nothing else left him in.

"You're one of my best detectives. I know you know that. You and Powell have no issues with confidence in your abilities."

It sounded like a compliment. Sort of.

"That's why I don't keep my eye on you two as much as I should. Because I know you can handle anything thrown your way."

He nodded, unsure of where this was going.

"I was informed this morning that Briella Colton has

been living with you for the past month. Care to explain why?"

Shit.

No, he did not.

Because he knew better than to get involved with someone connected to his cases. And he didn't care. He did it anyway because love made a person do crazy things.

"Well?"

That damn word again. He didn't know what his captain expected him to say.

"Is it true?"

Stromberg frowned. Meaning what? His captain didn't believe it.

"Where did this information come from?"

Captain Wilson shook his head, laughing with no inflection. "That's not how this works. And your lack of response tells me my answer. It's true. You're sleeping with a witness. In a murder investigation. Multiple murders."

Honestly, it was surprising his captain hadn't found out sooner. He'd gotten away with it for a whole month. And what a spectacular month it had been.

What it would continue to be. He'd pick Briella over his job any day.

"I'd like to know where you received this information from."

"I'd like my detective who never crosses a line to tell me why he did."

"I don't have an answer for that. Not one you'd like."

"I don't like anything about this." His captain sighed again, gesturing to his badge on his hip. "Gun and badge."

"I can't be pulled off this case."

His captain leaned forward, scowling. "You're going to be lucky if you even get your damn gun and badge back."

Stromberg stood up, grabbed his gun and badge, and laid them on the desk. He might never touch those two objects again.

But it wouldn't stop him from his end goal.

Finding the killer wreaking havoc on Briella's life.

13

BRIELLA SET her phone on the kitchen counter wondering if she should've responded differently. He was back to saying those three little words, and she wasn't sure how to express her feelings. Did she love Wyatt? He made her feel things she had never felt. Was that love? She had no clue.

"So?" Abby drawled, standing on the other side of the island.

Briella twirled around, offering a fake smile. She knew Abby saw right through it. If she was going to get through this evening without breaking down into a big blubbery mess then she had to pretend everything was okay.

"They found her. My neighbor."

There was no need to add that they found her dead. Abby knew. She hadn't been able to keep the desolation out of her tone of voice.

"Well, that's shitty."

Briella giggled with Abby, even though it wasn't funny. But the way she had expressed it, well, that deserved a chuckle. It felt good to release it. To let loose something happy instead of sad for once.

She clapped her hands, brimming from ear to ear. Because if she was going to pretend everything was hunky-dory, she was going all in with it. "Let's make some cookies!"

Abby's brow cocked as her lips formed a tentative smirk and drawled, "Yeah, let's do that."

"You hate baking?"

Abby laughed. "I have no idea. I don't bake. Just know they will taste disgusting if I help."

Briella nodded. "I don't bake either. So disgusting cookies coming right up."

Abby jumped with glee, getting into the moment as much as her. This wouldn't erase the pain as well as downing a whole bottle of whiskey would, but at least it would take her mind off the horror for a while. That's what she needed at the moment.

She grabbed her Bluetooth speaker, put on some funky tunes, then searched for a good chocolate chip recipe. They had ingredients spread out across the counters and a decent mess soon after. Abby kept popping chocolate chips into her mouth and Briella found that a great idea. Half the bag was gone before they even got to the part to add it to the dough.

"So if you don't normally bake, why are there chocolate chips in the cupboard?"

Briella shrugged. "You'd have to ask Wyatt. I didn't buy them." As she thought about it, she hadn't helped purchase any groceries since she moved in.

Moved in?

But she hadn't moved in. She still had her apartment—that she never went to anymore.

Her hand shook as she stirred the batter, a shiver running down her spine. Wow. No matter how much she wanted to ignore the obvious, she had moved in with him. She'd been back to her apartment to grab things now and again, but she couldn't remember the last time she slept inside it. What else could she say other than she had moved in? She'd had this internal conversation before with herself, but she couldn't lie to herself anymore. She and Wyatt were so entwined in each other's lives, she had to start admitting the hard truths.

"I need to use the bathroom. Want to take over?"

She knew Abby saw through her panic, no doubt wondering where it came from, but she was kind enough not to say anything. Abby took the spoon and Briella dashed out of the kitchen, nearly slamming the bathroom door as soon as she slid inside. She locked it for some unknown reason. Why would Abby come bother her?

Deep, heavy breaths attacked her as she took a seat on the toilet lid. Everything flooded her mind, overwhelmed her, causing her to bend over, throwing her head between her legs. The erratic breathing wouldn't lessen.

What was she doing?

Moving in with a man without talking about it. Not contributing to the household. Using him for his protection. Here he confessed his love, and she could do nothing in return. Not even express a tiny bit of affection.

Why did he put up with her? She was nothing but trouble waiting to happen. Someone out there was terrorizing her. Wanting to hurt her. Kill her. When it finally happened, where would that leave Wyatt? Nowhere but in tremendous pain.

If she left now, the blow would be easier on him.

He wouldn't be as devastated that he couldn't protect her.

Because honestly, she had a bad feeling about all of this. Why target her neighbor? Why kill her sister in the first place? Why wait a whole year to kill again? None of it made sense. Least of all who could be doing this. It had to be someone she knew. But as hard as she wracked her brain to think of someone she knew who could do something so heinous, nobody sprang to mind.

She sat up when a knock sounded on the door.

"You okay? You've been in here for almost fifteen minutes. At five, I thought you had to take a shit or something."

Briella snickered at Abby's attempt to lighten the mood. It worked.

"At ten minutes, I worried it was more than just consti-pation. Now at fifteen, it's making me truly worry. Do I need to call Stromy?"

Briella shot up from the toilet, flipped the lock, and swung open the door. "We've practically moved in together. When did that happen? We didn't even talk about it. He said I love you in his last text. It's not the first time he's said it either. I'm such a bitch that I can't even say a small I care about you in return."

Abby's eyes filled with sympathy, and that was the last thing Briella wanted to see. She wanted to slam the door shut, but Abby must've sensed her flight mode kicking in. Abby stepped forward, making her step back and letting her farther into the bathroom.

"When I met Tate, it was this all-consuming emotion that flooded my system. I didn't understand it. It was intense from the start. We were inseparable. We had sex on the first date. My love for him was immediate. It was scary as hell, considering I don't let people in easily. But he felt the same, and it made everything that I was feeling that much more real. That I wasn't creating things in my head."

Their situation was not even close to being the same. She met Wyatt over a year ago. She didn't even like him in the beginning. It had nothing to do with his personality. He was always professional and displayed his compassion toward her each time they spoke. It was more because he couldn't give her the answers she desperately sought. She blamed him for it. It was easier to put him as the bad guy than to put herself through all the guilt that she hadn't been there for her sister.

Abby must've sensed the confusion warping her features. "What I'm trying to say is that feeling all that chaos swarming you is normal. Being unsure and doubting yourself is not something you should panic about. I had that too. What scares you the most about falling for him? As soon as you answer that, everything will be a lot clearer."

Would it? She wasn't sure what the answer to that question was yet.

"What scared you the most about falling in love with Tate?"

Abby shivered, wrapping her arms around herself. "That I wouldn't be alone anymore. I'd been alone for so long, I didn't know how to let someone in. As soon as I gave in to that, to knowing that I didn't have to be alone anymore, it was so much easier to love him. To embrace what we were. If I lost him now, I know I'd die myself. He's my other half and I'd be lost without him."

Those strong words resonated with her. She feared she felt the same thing for Wyatt. She knew he'd be fraught with anguish if she left, but she feared for him every single day. Every time he walked out the door, she wondered if he would walk back in. He didn't exactly have the safest job. Dealing with the worst of the worst of society. Bringing monsters to justice, like the person who killed her sister, Flora, and now her neighbor.

She inhaled, then cringed. "What is that smell?"

Abby's eyes enlarged, then laughter burst free. "Shit! The cookies. I knew I'd suck at this."

They both rushed out of the bathroom, wrinkling their noses at the burnt smell perforating the air.

Abby grabbed a potholder and pulled the sheet of cookies out of the oven. Instead of looking golden brown and delicious, they were black and smelled like death. Fitting, since that's all that had been touching her life lately.

She blew out a breath, then shrugged. "Well, batch one isn't quite edible. We still have more dough to get this right."

She also had time to get it right with Wyatt. The killer hadn't gotten to her yet. That meant she needed to get her head on straight and figure out her feelings for him.

Before it was too late.

HE OPENED THE DOOR, smiling at the picture before him. Considering the day he had, it was hard to smile anymore.

"Well, how do they expect to keep each other safe if they're asleep?" Tate whispered, walking in behind him.

Stromberg knew it was a rhetorical question. There was no good answer to that. Abby and Briella were fast asleep on the couch. The TV blared with a reality show that made him roll his eyes. He didn't know how they could sleep with it on so loud.

"I'll see you tomorrow." Tate then scooped Abby up before she could even put her shoes on. She didn't protest and snuggled closer in his embrace.

Stromberg chuckled, then locked the door behind them. Instead of joining Briella on the couch where she still slept, he went to the kitchen where an odd smell emanated from. More laughter fell out at the mess before him. It felt so damn good to laugh. Ingredients covered the counter, flour even on the floor. Cookies sat on a wire wrack, piled high. Some were black, some looked edible. He picked up one of the cookies that looked more brown than black and took a bite. Not bad. It tasted like a chocolate chip cookie as much as it looked like one.

He finished the cookie, then proceeded to pick up the mess and toss the dishes in the dishwasher. Once finished, he grabbed a shower, because anytime he visited a crime scene he always needed a shower. He had to wash off the death that lingered everywhere.

When he walked back into the living room, the first thing he did was turn off the TV. Briella still didn't move at the loss of sound. He scooped her up and smiled at the way she wriggled in his arms as Abby had in Tate's. Then he walked her to the bedroom and laid her down. As soon as he hopped into his side of the bed, she was moving closer, wrapping her arms around him.

Contentment, for the first time, smothered him. Despite being benched at his job, all day he'd worried more about his idiotic behavior and texting he loved her. He knew that would send her into a panic, and yet he'd done it anyway. But had she gone into a panic? She didn't run. She stayed in his apartment. Even fell asleep, as if she felt secure in the fact he'd protect her.

Now, she was curled into his side. She didn't say anything, and if she had woken up from all the jostling he had done carrying her to the room, she didn't indicate it, so he chose to stay silent as well. He wasn't prepared to have any kind of serious talk tonight anyway. Too much had happened, and he knew once he told her, she'd blame herself. Might even leave him because of it.

Soon, he fell asleep with her.

Despite Briella next to him, he had trouble sleeping.

Nightmares plagued him. Flashes of blood soaking his bed. A mangled body that looked too eerily like Briella. Screams of anguish as she fought for her life. Laughter as the killer pounded into her body, her struggles useless against him.

"Wyatt!"

He flinched, popping open his eyes. Briella leaned over him, brushing his cheek.

"You were having a nightmare. Are you okay?"

Hell, no! It had been a horrifying nightmare. One he feared could come true if he didn't find this bastard soon.

He pulled her closer, steering her to relax her head on his chest. "I'm much better now."

Her hand brushed up and down his chest. "Do you want to talk about it?"

"Not really."

She delivered a few more strokes before whispering, "What did you find out tonight?"

He internally groaned. He didn't want to have that conversation right now either, but he understood her need to want the information. He managed to get some work done before being called to the captain's office like a kid being sent to the principal's office. Even after handing in his gun and badge, well, those two little things wouldn't stop him from his goal. He still worked alongside Tate today as if it hadn't happened. If anyone tattled on him...well, he was already in the hot seat. What did it matter if he added a little more water to that pot?

"Your security sucks in your apartment building. Despite having cameras up, they don't actually work, so we have no surveillance of the guy coming or going into the building. No forced entry, so she either knew the killer or he knows how to break in without leaving a trace. Most likely, he killed her last night." A slow breath released. "I don't have any good answers. Same as last time."

She leaned up again, another smooth hand caressing his cheek. "It's not your fault. You're doing the best you can."

But it wasn't good enough. And if something ended up happening to Briella, he'd never forgive himself.

"It's not your fault either. You know that, right?"

Because he knew she blamed herself as well.

"Why is he picking people I know? Well, besides Flora. I still can't recall if I've met her before."

"I don't know, but just because he is doesn't mean it's your fault." He snaked a hand around her neck. "Say you understand that. I don't want you blaming yourself."

A heavy sigh escaped her delectable lips before she finally nodded. "I'll try not to if you do too."

"Deal."

Then he crushed his mouth to hers, done with that topic. No more death on his mind. He needed to erase all those nasty images with something sweet and sensual. Briella knew what he wanted, deepening the kiss as she rolled on top of him.

He brushed his hands up her back, taking her shirt along with it. Then it was up and over her head and flung to the floor. He'd already gotten naked before climbing into bed, so nothing to remove for him. She shimmied until she had her sweats and underwear off, and instead of locking lips with him again, she slid down his body.

"Briella, you don't have..."

His words died as her mouth wrapped around his cock, taking him deep. A low groan filled the room, and everything emptied from his mind but the beautiful ministrations she was performing on him. Teeth scraping against his cock, then her sweet lips soothing the ache away. In and out she played with him. His hips matched the tune she was creating. The pleasure built fast, and he didn't want it to be over that soon.

"Baby, I need you. Not like this. Please, baby." His hands fiddled with her hair for her to stop, yet his hips betrayed his words as they continued to pump in rhythm with her mouth.

"Oh, baby, I'm so close. I want to be inside you," he growled, fisting her hair.

She moaned at the contact but kept on twisting her lips and stroking her tongue along the length of him. Then he came, the bliss bursting free. She sucked him dry until his entire body went limp.

Then she floated back up his chest, her hand running through his hair. "I'm sorry, were you saying something, Wyatt?"

A sexy grin punctured his lips right before he kissed her breathless. He flipped her effortlessly, laughing along with her excited giggles.

"My turn."

Her hands attached to his ass as a saucy smile appeared. "No, I want to feel you inside me. I'm calling the shots tonight, and I demand you put that thick cock inside me. I know you want to."

Damn but he did. He could feel himself getting hard at the naughty way the words left her mouth.

"Are you sure?" he asked with a teasing grin, knowing this was what she wanted—the verbal teasing before they came together in glorious ecstasy.

That sassy smile of hers grew even wider. "Don't make me smack your ass." Then she proceeded to slap his ass hard. "Or rake my nails down your back." Her nails did just that, sending anticipatory goose bumps down his spine. "Or wrap my mouth around that thick cock again."

She wiggled as if she'd be able to escape. He held her still and thrust deep inside instead. She moaned deliriously, arching her back. "Deeper, Wyatt."

So he followed her commands. Pumping deeper, then harder as she cried out her demands. He could feel the pleasure rising again, the need to claim her as he swelled inside.

The heat in the room grew. Her sweet moans mingled with his hearty groans. Nothing existed between them but the desire. He felt the urge to profess his love bubbling up his throat, but he held it back. She might freak, and he never wanted this to end. He knew she'd run when she found out what happened to him at work.

Her nails dug into his ass, urging him on. Deeper, harder, faster. Then she clenched around him, screaming his name. He kept on pumping, needing a bit more time. The erotic sounds spilling from her lips was what sent him over the edge a second time.

His body was completely spent now. He had enough energy to move off her body and pull her into his arms, but that was it. Any other kind of movement would be impossible. He placed a tender kiss on her forehead as he closed his eyes.

"Wyatt?"

"Yeah, baby," he whispered, feeling the sleep wanting to take over. He sensed the nightmares wouldn't return anymore after what they had just done.

"I love you."

His eyes darted open. She was staring at him with a slight fear tinting her eyes. Why? Those three words were something he'd been dying to hear for the longest time.

He brushed a hand across her cheek and then through her dark locks, fisting a handful. "I love you too."

"There's no need for two apartments...right?"

He could feel her heartbeat, which was rapidly mirroring his own. "There's not."

Hallelujah, she was officially moving in with him. What was happening? Was he still dreaming? Was this part of the nightmare and he'd wake up tomorrow and realize it never happened?

"Okay, then. Good night." Then she swiped another kiss and closed her eyes.

He could do nothing but lay there staring at her, wondering if he dreamt it all.

14

SHE LET the water hit her back, the hot pelts working the kinks she could still feel. Wyatt had promised her a back rub and...

And she'd received that disgusting video. While she hadn't gotten that beloved back rub she'd been looking forward to, they had come together in magical bliss last night. She'd insist on a back rub tonight after they packed up some of her apartment.

He'd woken first, jumping in the shower, unaware she had woken up too. She pretended to be asleep when he came out of the shower and didn't hop out of bed until he left the room. There was no definitive reason why she feigned sleep. He normally didn't jump out of bed right away without waking her, so she sensed he wanted time alone. She smelled the makings of coffee by the time she reached the shower.

It was silly to feel nervous after what she said, but his odd behavior this morning made her so nervous she wanted to puke. But the most important thing was she *had* said it. The awkwardness could disappear. They loved each other, and they were officially moving in together. She never thought she'd ever find someone like Wyatt and want to build a life with them. But she had, and now that she'd accepted it for what it was. She was jumping in with both feet. No hesitation. No looking. Just flinging herself into it wholeheartedly.

Knowing she was stalling, she finally cut the water off and stepped out of the shower. She dressed, blow-dried her hair, and applied makeup all in a decent time. She wanted to pat herself on the back. She found Wyatt in the kitchen, slapping some butter on toast. The smile he sent her way when he met her gaze was enough to make her insides flutter and her knees go weak. Good thing the counter was close-by because she needed it to keep her upright. Maybe she misinterpreted his behavior this morning and nothing was wrong between them.

"Good morning. Coffee's done, and I'm almost finished with the toast. Eggs are on the plates already."

They didn't always make breakfast for each other. Sometimes, a bowl of cereal worked well. Other times they stopped at a cafe to grab a quick bite. But she decided she liked him making her something to get the day started. She loved the fact she'd convinced him having breakfast was a good start to any day.

He pushed the plate closer after setting the toast by the eggs. She slid into his embrace instead of taking the food.

"How thoughtful of you." Then she kissed him, her mind flying to the previous evening when they made love so fervently.

His arm around her waist tightened, deepening the kiss until her low moan entered the space. "Baby, we shouldn't."

Hmm. Why not? "Of course we can," she whispered

against his lips, feeling the smile that graced his handsome face.

"We need to talk."

Four little words, but so brutal.

She stepped back, missing his warm arm holding her close, but she wanted distance for this conversation. What could have gone wrong in the space of...well, since she said she loved him in return? The toast begged for her to take a bite, so she obliged before speaking.

Then, because she knew she wouldn't like what he had to say, she decided she'd steer the conversation to something she wanted to talk about.

"I'm going to work today. You can drop me off there."

Wyatt frowned, crossing his arms. "Are you sure that's a good idea?"

"Do I look hysterical to you? Do I look despondent or not capable of doing my job?"

His brows puckered as if he were pondering all those questions. The audacity of him. As if she were falling apart right before his eyes.

"I thought you'd want some time..."

She waved her hand for him to continue, dying to hear his thoughts. "Go on. Time to what? Go crazy thinking about that...that video! I need to occupy my time with something other than what the killer might do next. There's no need for me to take off work. I need the money."

"What for?"

This time her brows drew low, deciphering his odd question. "For stuff. For half the rent here. For food in the cupboards. I don't know. For sexy lingerie, even though I'm not sure you deserve it right now."

His confusion vanished and panic took its place. He

stepped forward and pulled her into his arms. She could feel the anxiety coursing through his veins.

"I wasn't dreaming last night."

She brushed his forehead, smoothing out the wrinkles —and the tension. Then she swooped her hand through his dark locks. "You thought you dreamt me saying I love you?"

Was that what he wanted to talk about?

"It had crossed my mind this morning I created it in my head because I wanted to hear it so badly. I don't want to lose you."

"I'm right here, Wyatt. I'm not going anywhere." Her brow rose as she pursed her lips. "Unless you continue to act like an idiot. I'm not moving in unless I help around here. I haven't been contributing and that's not okay."

"I don't mind taking care of you. I love doing it."

"Ditto," she replied, running another soft touch through his hair. She loved the way his eyes flared with desire every time she did. "So after work, because I'm working today, we can go to my apartment and start packing."

A wide smile spread across his lips. "I do love the sound of that plan." Part of the happiness slipped away. "I don't want you to push yourself at work though. Take it easy."

"I wasn't physically hurt, Wyatt. Why are you stressing so much about me going to work?"

His hands on her back pressed harder, as if that would help get his message across better. "I don't know how to explain what I'm feeling. I just know that I'm going to worry like hell about you. About this killer...getting his hands on you."

"Well, unfortunately, we've established he can get anywhere. In public. In private. I refuse to let him control my life. I will not hide from him."

"Don't make yourself a damn target either."

"I would never."

She wasn't dumb or asking for trouble. She only wanted to keep living her life as if nothing were wrong. Letting that psychotic bastard rule her life would never happen. Never!

They quickly ate, downed the coffee, and then left. She saw the tension return in his features when he dropped her off. Not even the energetic kiss she gave him helped to remove any of it. She'd have to try harder tonight to lessen his worry.

The diner was busy, as usual for a morning, so she didn't have time to chat with Beth until the rush died down.

"I thought you weren't coming in. You doing okay?"

She nodded, grateful to have her mind on something as mundane as taking orders and dealing with people who wanted a good bite to eat. Well, as good as one could get from this place with mediocre food.

"I'd rather be here. What good is it to sit at home and think about that gross video?" She shivered, unable to stop it. "Wyatt and Tate found the woman. She's dead."

Beth's hand flew to her mouth, a sob tearing out. "That's horrible."

Briella put a hand on Beth's shoulder. "I wanted to let you know, but I don't want to talk about it."

"Of course not." Though Beth's eyes betrayed her. She wanted to know more, but Briella wasn't going to indulge her. She came to work to get her mind off it, not think about it even more.

They parted ways, getting back to work.

The small pain in her lower back was starting to give her fits again. When she stopped at the table where one of her regulars sat, she saw his eyes flicker to her hand on her back before she had removed it.

"Everything okay?" he asked in the same smooth tone he always used.

Eugene was a quiet sort. They didn't chat about anything too personal, not like Darlene who loved to chat about her kids and the trouble they could get into. He always had something nice to say, complimenting her on occasion. Not in a flirtatious way. His eyes never lingered longer than they should. He didn't raise his voice or get angry about anything. Even the time Johnny burned his chicken. She would've raised a stink about it. How do you burn chicken and then literally send it out? Tonya, another waitress, had taken the order before she could grab it and delivered it. She had reamed Tonya out for touching her orders *and* for giving a customer anything burnt. Overall, Eugene was a kind man, who always used the same tone of voice. Pleasant and charming.

"I've been having this back pain for a few days. I should stretch it or work out or something. I will be demanding a back rub from my boyfriend tonight, at the very least." She chuckled, then cleared her throat when she swore she saw a flash of irritation in Eugene's eyes.

Right. They didn't talk personal stuff with each other. Well, he had asked if everything was okay. It was his fault for asking.

"I'm sorry to hear you're in pain. I like to get those patches with the medication sometimes. They work wonders to clear up the ache in no time."

She smiled, glad to hear his normal delicate tone. Perhaps she misinterpreted his look moments before. "I'll look into that. I never thought to do that. I don't even know what I did to aggravate it."

Wyatt had a wonderful bed; it was like sleeping on a bed of clouds. She'd picked up the laundry basket, carried it to the hallway where the washer and dryer were tucked away in a tiny closet, and set it down. It was when she sat down on the couch to binge the rest of the reality TV show she loved that she felt the small ache. Maybe the load of laundry had been too big. Too much for her to carry. It hadn't hurt while carrying it, but that was the only thing she could think that had done it.

"Anyway, you don't want to hear about my aches and pains. What can I get you today?"

"I never mind chatting with you about anything. I truly am sorry to hear you're hurting." His smile appeared genuine. She appreciated his thoughtfulness. "I would love the turkey BLT. Fries are fine, and some mayo on the side."

"You got it."

She walked away, jumping, even a tiny squeak left her mouth when she nearly smacked right into Bryan.

"I am so sorry. I didn't mean to get in your way. I was going to grab the chair at the counter, and I didn't expect you to turn so abruptly."

The smile on his face should've eased her discomfort, but all it did was raise her suspicions. Because seriously, what was he doing in the diner where she worked? Her sister's cemetery, which was near the cafe where she first saw him a month ago, was nowhere near this diner. She'd never seen him visit here before.

"How are you? Funny running into you again," he said with laughter.

She didn't join in. Rude, yeah, but she didn't have the patience for this kind of shit today.

"Why are you here?"

He looked puzzled, and she wasn't buying his innocent act. "To eat. It is a diner."

"Why this diner?"

"It's near where I work. I've been here before." He frowned. "What's with the twenty questions? Is it not okay I eat here?"

And maybe she was blowing things out of proportion. He'd startled her and it made her panic.

"No, of course, you can eat here." She flashed a fake smile and swept a hand toward the counter. "Have a seat and I'll be right with you. I have to put another customer's order in."

His smarmy, innocent smile appeared once again. "Sounds good. We can catch up since you're here. It is nice to see you again."

Well, it wasn't in her eyes, and she had no intention of doing any personal chatting with him. She'd rather take a seat with Eugene and do that instead. She didn't get the icky, creepy vibes from him.

Matter of fact...

What an idiot!

She should've thought of this a long time ago. A whole month ago.

She darted into the kitchen, passed off Eugene's order, and pulled out her phone.

> Bryan Lauder. Look into him. He's an old friend of Dawn's. I've now seen him twice in the past month when I haven't seen him in more than a year...since Dawn's funeral. It's weird.

> Where did you see him? Are you okay?

> He's at the diner right now. It's filled with people, so I'm fine. He gives me the creeps. I thought I'd pass along his name.

Yes, I want to know about anyone who gives you the creeps. I'm on it.

Which she knew he'd be. Wyatt would never stop until he caught this killer. For that, she'd always be thankful. For his tenaciousness when it came to his job.

Oh, and I love you. Be careful around him.

I love you too.

Be careful around him. She could do that. The knife sitting near the edge of the counter disappeared behind her shirt. Weird, yeah, if anyone saw it. But she already felt a hundred times safer knowing she had a weapon at her disposal if need be.

Bring it on, asshole. You're not getting me without a fight.

"BASED on the angry scowl you're wearing, whoever texted you didn't have anything nice to say," Tate drawled from the driver's seat as they sat outside Kelly's apartment building.

They'd interviewed a few of Kelly's friends and family, not garnering anything too helpful yet. Tate always introduced them, flashing his badge since Stromberg didn't currently have one. He was skating such a thin line right now. Working when he shouldn't be. Lying to his captain.

Lying to Briella.

He should've mentioned his suspension to her. That Internal Affairs was looking at him. Hell, someone could be on his tail now. He was an idiot for continuing to work the case, and yet, he couldn't stop himself. Not even Tate had tried to dissuade him.

Whoever this killer was they were good at everything. Hiding their face, breaking and entering, being quiet while they raped and slaughtered women. It all made Stromberg sick to his stomach, to the point he wanted to vomit. That's exactly why he couldn't walk away from this case.

"Briella." He passed his phone across the way, too agitated by what she wrote to speak it out loud.

Tate nodded, then started tapping away at the computer in the vehicle. He tapped the screen when he had the information he wanted. "Bryan Lauder. No criminal record. Not even a parking ticket. He had an alibi on the night of Dawn's death. He was seen leaving a bar around the time she was murdered."

"Yeah, but that bar was only three blocks away from Dawn's apartment. He had time to get there, do the deed, and to the gym where he worked out. Isn't that where he said he went afterward?"

Tate had a good memory as much as him. He knew the case from top to bottom. Because it was important to Stromberg, which made it important to him as well. "Yep. There's about two hours between the time he left the bar to going to the gym. Nothing is noted about why it took him so long to get from point A to point B."

"They were childhood friends. I didn't get a weird vibe from him." Stromberg leaned back in his seat, rubbing his chin. "But I don't like that he's suddenly appearing in Briella's life. Especially if she never saw him this much before."

"It is odd. It doesn't make him a killer."

Stromberg narrowed his eyes as he sat up. "You discrediting Briella's gut feeling, asshole?"

"I didn't say that. Just playing devil's advocate, jackass."

Tate twisted the key in the ignition. "Let's go have a chat with him."

He didn't need to be told twice. They arrived at the diner thirty minutes later. The bell above the door jingled, and he locked eyes with Briella right away. She was helping a couple in the far left corner. They headed to the counter and waited less than a minute before she joined them.

His first greeting was a delicious kiss. His second was a smile and a short hello.

"What are you doing here?" she asked with suspicious eyes, though the gentle grin on her lips said she wasn't mad about their visit.

"We wanted to chat with Bryan." Stromberg glanced around the diner, not seeing the man in question.

She folded her arms, her smile disappearing. "He left five minutes ago."

"Well, he wasn't here long. That's weird," Tate commented.

Her shoulders lifted up, then dipped down. "Not really. He said he works close-by, so he was only here for lunch. It's not like he could linger."

"How did it go while he was here?"

"Fine. I didn't chat much with him, even though he tried to talk with me. It's been busy today." She leaned into him, brushing her lips against his one more time. "So I can't chat with you long either. I didn't mean to make you rush here. That's not why I sent the text."

"You have a weird feeling, I'm following up on it immediately." He wrapped his hand around her neck, closing his eyes as he pressed his forehead to hers. "I love you so damn much, baby. I will not ignore something that makes you uncomfortable."

Her hands attached to his hips and squeezed. He felt the fear in the touch, but also her appreciation that he took what she said seriously.

Then her hands shifted around and she popped her head up. "I don't feel your gun. I always feel that thing attached to your hip."

Well, shit.

Not a great time to confess what happened.

"Wyatt?"

He produced a smile he didn't feel. "We'll talk about it tonight. I should go before your customers start grumbling." He snatched another kiss before letting her go. "He comes back again, call me the second you see his face."

She frowned but didn't stop him from leaving. What a coward he was!

"You didn't tell her yet?"

Stromberg slammed his door. "I don't know how to tell her. If Captain Wilson knows I'm still working this case..." He sighed. "Maybe I should stop."

"And maybe we should pay this asshole Bryan a visit."

Or they could do that. Tate was not a good partner in the sense of upholding what was right and what was wrong. What a damn bad influence he was.

Bryan worked four blocks away from the diner. He hadn't lied about that part. He worked for a law firm. A defense attorney. How interesting. When they asked to speak to him, they had to wait twenty minutes as he was in a meeting with a client. A small part of Stromberg enjoyed the spark of fear that touched his eyes when he met them in the lobby.

"How can I help you, Detective, um..." He snapped his fingers. "You're going to have to remind me of your last name. I know you're the one working on Dawn's case, but that's it."

"Detective Stromberg." He tossed his hand lazily toward

Tate. "This is Detective Powell. We have a few questions, if you don't mind."

"Sure. Follow me." He led them to a conference room where they all took a seat at the end of a long table. "How can I help? Has there been a lead in Dawn's murder?"

Stromberg almost believed his sincerity and innocence, until Briella's scared text punctured his brain.

"There have been two more murders that mirror Dawn's."

Bryan's eyes rounded, the shock hard to fake. Were they barking up the wrong tree? "That's awful. I saw Briella today. She didn't mention that."

Tate cleared his throat. "Why would she?"

"I mean, her sister..." Bryan shrugged, shifting in his seat as if uncomfortable. "How can I help? I don't understand why you want to speak to me."

Stromberg smiled, and it wasn't in a pleasant way. "Take a look at these photos and please tell me if you recognize either woman."

He slid his phone toward Bryan after finding the picture of Flora. Bryan's quick shake of his head said he didn't. Then he showed a picture of Kelly. There was a flash of surprise, as if he knew her, then another shake of his head to confirm he hadn't. Why lie if he knew her?

"Are you sure you don't know either woman?" Stromberg asked, taping the screen where Kelly's face glared at Bryan.

"No. Did they die exactly like Dawn? Those poor women. Their families." Bryan groaned, placing his hands over his face.

Stromberg wasn't buying this distraught act. Bryan knew Kelly. He saw through the lie right away.

"Briella has had a few threats sent to her."

Stromberg snapped his head at Tate, surprised he decided to divulge that information. They hadn't chatted about whether they'd bring Briella up. It would be obvious she told them Bryan had stopped by if they did. If he was the killer, he didn't want to antagonize him and trigger him to retaliate against her sooner than he planned. Because there was no doubt in his mind, whoever this killer was, they wanted to hurt Briella as much as they had the other three victims.

"By the killer?" The confusion on Bryan's face looked sincere. Again.

"Yes." Tate could be a man of few words, but it was generally the hard, discerning look on his face that had people squirming in their seats. Just as Bryan was doing right then.

"I'm beginning to think you two suspect me of something here." There was a short quiver in his voice. "Do I need a lawyer?"

Well, they were in the perfect place for him to grab one and join them in the room.

But that was the last thing Stromberg wanted him to do. "Do you want a lawyer? We're only chatting here."

"I get the sense I'm a suspect. So I don't think I should say anything else."

"Are you following Briella?" Stromberg chose to ignore what he had said.

"No! Why would you think that?"

"You've been two places where she's been now, when in the past year you hadn't seen her once. Now we have two more dead women, and she's getting threats. You knew Dawn *very well*," Tate emphasized the last two words. "So when we ask if you're following Briella, it's a damn serious question."

Bryan pressed his lips together, his eyes narrowing. Gone was the scared, innocent act he'd been portraying. "I'm done answering your questions. If you have any more, you can speak to my lawyer. He's right down the hallway."

Stromberg pulled his wallet out and then stopped. He'd had his badge taken away. He kept getting more involved in the case. Tate sensed his struggles, dug his wallet out, and slid his card toward Bryan.

"Give your lawyer my number to set up a time to chat today. We will need to verify your alibi for the last two murders. And take a deeper look at your alibi when Dawn was murdered. It doesn't take two hours to get from the bar you were at to the gym like you said you did. Also, who has a few drinks and then goes to work out? That's odd in and of itself." Tate stood up.

Stromberg was grateful he'd taken over, but that didn't mean he'd stay completely silent in all aspects. His face was as hard as granite as he said, "You will stay away from Briella. You will not go to the diner where she works. You will not pop up anywhere she happens to be. If I find out you have, I'll arrest you for stalking." With the badge he didn't have! But whatever. The asshole didn't know that.

A wide smirk grew on Bryan's face. "I don't happen to see a badge strapped to your hip like your partner. Are you sure you can arrest me?"

What. The. Hell.

"Keep up the attitude and watch me do it." Then he walked out of the room before he did something stupid, like punch the asshole in the face.

They were silent for a few beats in the car when Tate spoke first. "He looks suspicious and it fits a bit for him to be the killer."

Stromberg turned his head, meeting his gaze and seeing

the answer to the question he was about to ask. "But you don't think he's our guy?"

"No."

Yeah, he didn't even know why he had asked. It wasn't what he wanted to hear.

"I don't know if I agree. What about that bit about my badge?"

Tate shrugged. "It isn't on your hip. The guy is observant."

"Well, I'm not scratching him off the suspect list yet."

They had so much to do, he didn't even know where to start. Briella's life depended on it. This killer wasn't going to stop until he had what he wanted.

Briella dead.

15

THE NEWSPAPER CRINKLED as she wrapped another plate, then set it in the box. Wyatt had picked her up from work and, despite knowing he had a lot on his plate and wanted to keep working, he said he was finished for the night. They grabbed Chinese on the way to her apartment, ate quickly, and got right down to business. She said she wanted to start in the kitchen. She didn't need all the dishes, utensils, pots, and pans she had, but some were sentimental. The rest could be donated.

"You haven't said how your chat with Bryan went yet?"

She'd waited patiently all evening since the moment he picked her up from the diner, but she was done waiting. She needed to know.

Wyatt paused putting the cookie sheet she had decided to get rid of into the box. "He didn't say anything useful. He asked for a lawyer. His lawyer called us, and we set up an appointment with him for tomorrow."

"Is that normal?" Her hand tightened around the plate she had picked up before asking the question that had been gnawing at her all night. "Isn't that suspicious?"

"It's common for people who are suspects—and also innocent," he emphasized, "to ask for a lawyer. It doesn't necessarily mean he did it."

"So we don't think he did it?"

Wyatt rubbed his chin. "I have no idea. I don't like the gut feeling I get from him, but Tate's thinking he's not our guy. I don't like that he gives you the creeps."

Yeah, well, she wasn't sure what to think about her gut anymore. Eugene, toward the end of his meal, had started giving her the heebie-jeebies too. He'd asked again if she was okay, noting how she'd been uncomfortable when Bryan had been there. Then noticing when Wyatt had arrived and the agitation between them. Why was he staring at her? Why did he care? He was a customer, she was the waitress. They chatted about mundane things, not about how she was feeling. She gave him an "I'm fine" response and left it at that. It wasn't his business how she felt.

Or maybe she was starting to doubt any man she came across. They couldn't all be bad.

Wyatt sensed her anxiety, rounded the island standing between them, and pulled the plate from her grasp. It had been a good thing too because any more pressure on it and she would've broken it in her hands. Her hand from the whiskey bottle incident healed well, and she didn't need more stitches in her future. Once was enough!

"What's going on in that beautiful head of yours? I can sense something else is bothering you."

"I'm losing my mind. I'm suspecting every man I speak to."

His brows drew low as his hands gripped her hips. "Who else is bothering you?"

She shook her head. "He didn't bother me. I just got uncomfortable for a moment."

The way he stared at her said she'd better tell him everything, no matter how trivial she might think it was. So she relayed the entire encounter with Eugene.

"Do you know his last name? How often does he come into the diner?"

"Pretty regularly. About two to three times a week. It's usually for lunch, like Bryan had today. He works near the diner as well. Umm..." She blew out a breath, trying to remember what he did. "I think it's the health shop nearby. You know they sell vitamins and all that healthy crap."

He chuckled at her description, knowing she was a junk nut more than anything else. So was he, so he wasn't one to judge. He loved his sweets more than anything.

"Look, I've never had a weird feeling about him before. Now that I think about it, it was kind of him to make sure I was okay. Bryan did set me off-kilter showing up like that. Bryan gives me the creeps more than Eugene does."

"I'd still like to look into him. I need a last name. I'll figure it out tomorrow."

And that, Bri knew he'd do without a problem. When Wyatt got something on his mind, it was hard to get him to leave it alone.

His hands traveled from her hips to her back, pulling her closer. Then he frowned as his hand fiddled with her shirt before pulling it up and sliding the knife she had hidden there out of her waistband.

The level of shock on his face surprised her, and she wasn't sure why. She had a right to defend herself if the need arose.

"Why do you have a knife tucked in the back of your pants?"

"I told you, Bryan made me uncomfortable. I saw it sitting on the counter in the kitchen at work and I grabbed it. It made me feel better throughout the day." Her eyes glided to the sharp device as Wyatt set it on the counter. "I forgot it was there. It felt like a part of me after a while."

He framed her face, his eyes intense. "I don't want you ever to feel unsafe. If carrying around a knife helps, then do it. It took me by surprise, but I get it. Do you think you could use it on someone?"

She shivered and his hands strengthened their grip on her cheeks. "I don't want to find out."

Then he smoothed his hands up and through her hair, yanking her to his chest where she held on for dear life.

"I don't want you to ever find out either. I will catch this bastard. I'm looking hard at Bryan, and now I'll add Eugene to the list. I will look into anyone that makes you even the slightest bit uncomfortable. So if you have an odd feeling, you need to tell me right away. Got it?"

"Yes." The short word came out muffled because she had her face mushed to his chest. But she loved the close feeling and how safe she felt cocooned in his arms.

"Maybe this is a good time to tell me why you didn't have your gun on you today. Or tonight either."

He stiffened.

She pulled away.

He let her.

"What are you keeping from me?"

Wyatt ran a hand through his hair, slumping against the counter behind him. "My captain found out we're together. I shouldn't be dating someone involved in one of my cases. I had to hand in my gun and badge yesterday."

She didn't know what to think or feel at the moment. He'd lied to her. Withheld the truth.

"It doesn't matter what happened. I haven't stopped working the case."

"Wyatt!" What was he thinking?! "You love your job. You shouldn't be risking it all for me."

He shot up from the counter, grasping her shoulders. "So I should walk away from you? I should pretend I don't love you? Not going to happen. I promised I'd find your sister's killer and I will not be breaking that promise. I also recall telling you that you're mine. Nothing is going to take you away from me. Not even my job."

"It's who you are," she whispered, hating that it had come to this. Another thing her fault. Another thing she'd caused because of her actions.

"I don't want to argue about this. It happened. It's over."

"It's far from over."

His grip on her shoulders tightened, then relaxed. He brushed his hands down her arms until he found her hands, linking fingers with her. "You are the most important thing in my life. I don't know how else to show or tell you that. Please, let's not argue about this."

They could agree on one thing at least. She didn't want to argue about it. So for now, she'd let it go. But if he thought she'd continue to ignore it, he was wrong.

"Fine."

By the tight reply, he knew the issue would crop back up.

They eventually pulled apart and got back to work. She slid the knife behind her back once again because she didn't want to lose it or mistake it for one of the utensils she was giving away. Most of the kitchen was taken care of when they decided to take a break for the evening.

The trip to Wyatt's apartment made her sleepy. After taking a shower, she hopped into bed, not up for doing anything else. Even watching her beloved reality TV shows. Wyatt joined her.

They fell asleep easily. Unlike last night, Wyatt experienced no nightmares. They didn't wake up until the alarm went off. He had set it with extra time to love her body thoroughly, which she had no objection to. He showered first, and when she finished getting ready, he had breakfast once again waiting for her. This time a bagel and a bowl of strawberries.

She gulped down some coffee first.

"I'll be busy today." He rolled his eyes at his own words because he was busy every day. "But call me if you need me. I don't care what it is."

She stepped closer, brushing his bearded cheek. "Don't worry about me. I will be careful, and I will call you if anything is weird. I promise. Why will you be busy?"

The incredulous look he gave her said that was a stupid question. "I told you, I'm not stopping just because I don't have a badge strapped to my hip."

"You could get into even more trouble. I'm not worth—"

He crushed his mouth to hers, drowning out everything else she wanted to say. "If I ever hear you try to say something like that again, I'll spank your ass so hard, you'll feel it into next week."

She grinned, knowing it irked him. "Promises, promises."

"Briella..."

She lost the spark in her eyes as she fisted his shirt. "Don't get into any more trouble. Please be careful today."

"I'm always careful. My job is not something I want you to worry about."

He snatched a kiss, then reached over and picked up the knife she'd carried around all day yesterday. His warm hand on her back set her body on fire as it always did. Then the coldness of the knife sent a shiver up her spine as he tucked it into its spot.

"Keep it on you at all times. It was a good idea to arm yourself. I should get you some pepper spray instead." He cupped her cheeks, leaning closer. "Don't cut yourself."

She giggled, despite it not being funny. "I'll be careful. I promise. Now kiss me, then take me to work."

He followed orders, giving her the deepest, most erotic kiss to date. She wanted to call in sick and spend the day in bed from the kiss alone. Sadly, she knew it couldn't happen. Even with him being suspended, she knew it wouldn't stop him from working the case. Nothing would keep them in this apartment today. He was on a mission.

She ate on the way to the diner, stole another kiss from Wyatt before pasting on a smile, and greeted her first customer.

Whoever was out there trying to terrorize her and kill women, she would not let it affect her. She was stronger than that.

In the end, she'd win against him.

THEIR MEETING with Bryan and his lawyer wasn't until one o'clock, but it didn't mean they didn't have other things to take care of.

He couldn't risk going to the precinct, being suspended and all, so Tate met him at the diner. He drove as they tried to find the health store Briella had mentioned.

They found it two blocks away—Supple-mental Health for You. Stromberg found the name of the store fitting and creative. Mental health was as important to a healthy lifestyle as was eating right and consuming the correct vitamins.

Like the diner, a bell rang as they opened the door. A

guy behind the counter smiled as they approached. He didn't look familiar, but then again, Stromberg didn't pay a whole lot of attention when he walked into the diner. His focus was always on Briella. He'd have to rectify that mistake and be more aware of his surroundings when he visited her.

"Can I help you, gentlemen?" the guy asked with a peppy tune that grated on Stromberg's nerves. He didn't much care for health nuts.

"We're looking for Eugene."

The guy nodded as if that weren't an odd request at all. "He's in the back. I'll get him for you."

Tate turned around and leaned against the counter, folding his arms. "He must hand out his card or something. Did he ever give Briella a card to stop by and shop here?"

Stromberg shook his head. "Not that I'm aware of. I'll ask to confirm."

Eugene came out less than a minute later, a smile on his face. It died the instant he recognized him.

"How can I help you, detective?"

Tate swiveled back around, his brow cocking.

Stromberg was surprised himself. He hadn't introduced himself to him or the other guy. "How do you know I'm a detective?"

Eugene eyed him up and down and did the same to Tate. "It's not hard to decipher. I also know you visit Briella on occasion, and I have seen your badge on those occasions."

Hmm.

Stromberg didn't like that. The fact he was paying attention to Briella a lot more than she realized.

"Well, then your bright deductive skills should be telling you why I'm here."

Instead of confirming, Eugene frowned. "Not really, no."

The bell above the door rang and two men walked inside, prompting Eugene to gesture toward the back where he had appeared from. "Why don't we chat back here?"

It didn't matter to Stromberg where they talked. But he wasn't leaving until he was satisfied with the answers.

He led them to a room that had a fridge, sink, and a large round table. Then they all sat at the table. Eugene looked relaxed in his seat, but his eyes held a bit of panic. That's what Stromberg planned to latch onto.

"How well do you know Briella?" he asked, matching Eugene's relaxed posture in the chair. Tate sat rigidly next to him, but that was a normal trait of his. The dude rarely relaxed.

"I mean, not that well. I eat at the diner quite a bit. They have good food and decent prices. I'd spend the same amount buying groceries and making lunch to bring to work. I like the walk as well. It's good to get my steps in. She normally serves me."

Stromberg's eyes narrowed at the double meaning. Though Eugene's expression didn't say he was trying to insinuate a sexual meaning.

"Did you know her sister was murdered last year?"

Eugene nodded. "I heard about it in the news. I didn't realize it was her sister until I heard her talking about it with another waitress at the diner. She didn't work at the diner when it happened, otherwise I would've offered my condolences at the time. I felt weird offering it now because it's rude to listen in on conversations. I didn't mean to be rude."

"And where were you the night she was murdered?" Tate asked, flipping open the small notepad he had pulled out and offered the night of the murder to help refresh Eugene's memory.

He blew out an exasperated breath, shrugging. "I don't

remember. It was over a year ago. Probably what I do most nights. I work, I head to the gym, I go home."

"No friends? No girlfriend? You don't do anything other than work, go to the gym, and go home?" Tate asked with a sliced tone.

"Well, yeah, I have friends. No girlfriend, but yeah, I go out with my friends on occasion. But she was murdered on a Wednesday. I don't typically go out on a Wednesday. So I imagine I was home."

"Alone?" Stromberg added.

Eugene nodded, his lips pressed in a thin line. "Yes, alone. Obviously, that isn't helping my case at the moment." He leaned forward, his brows dipping. "Why am I a suspect?"

Tate flipped the page in his notepad, ignoring the question. "Two more women in the last month have been murdered in the same way as Dawn was." He rattled off those dates. "How about an alibi for them?"

Eugene expressed his annoyance with another hard breath. "Same as Dawn's. I leave work at five, go to the gym for an hour, and I'm home by seven."

"Which gym do you go to?" Stromberg asked. It would be easy enough to verify he was there at those times. All three women were murdered in the early evening. Time of death between six and ten o'clock, all varying a few degrees.

"Weights and More. It's not far from here. My apartment is a few more blocks away from the gym. I walk everywhere. I like walking."

They asked a few more questions, not garnering anything else useful. But Stromberg wouldn't be satisfied until he spoke with the gym. Even then, he had no solid alibi after seven. He'd screwed himself being home alone.

They thanked him and proceeded to leave.

"Did Briella say something about me? I would never hurt her."

Stromberg turned around in the doorway, noting the hurtful look in Eugene's eyes. "I would find somewhere else to eat."

Then he left. Eugene would do well to listen to his demand. Stromberg wouldn't be responsible for his actions if Eugene ignored him.

They verified that Eugene had been at the gym for every murder. Lucky for him, they had a system where members swiped a card to get in, noting the time. He was a regular, so the workers were even able to swear on a bible if they had to that he always stayed a full hour. So his time could be accounted for from five to seven. But what about afterward?

An hour before the meeting with Bryan's lawyer would've commenced, Stromberg got a call from his captain. Back into his office he went.

He sat rigid, waiting for the final blow to his career. He knew it had been dumb to continue to work the case but nothing—not even a fatal natural disaster—would've stopped him from finding the killer.

"You don't listen very well, do you?"

He figured that was a rhetorical question, so he didn't respond.

His captain grabbed an envelope sitting on his desk and pulled out a piece of paper. He unfolded it and set it in front of him.

I would like to bring to your attention that Detective Wyatt Stromberg is currently living and sleeping with one of the witnesses in his case. Briella Colton.

Stromberg eyed the envelope, noting nothing but Captain Wilson written on the front. No return address or even a stamp. The letter itself was computer-generated. No writing of any kind.

"How was it delivered?"

And why didn't his captain show him this letter yesterday before he suspended him? Why show him now?

"In my mailbox here. I've already looked at the surveillance video and I saw the man who delivered the letter; however, his face was shielded. He kept his head down, indicating he knew where the cameras are located. No prints on the envelope or the letter."

"So you got an anonymous tip about Briella."

It wasn't a question at all. But he had to voice it. He'd been outed by some unknown individual.

"He's playing more games with us. This time with me."

Captain Wilson agreed with a sharp nod. "You're stepping on his territory. This killer doesn't like you around Briella all the time."

"Which is why I'm around her all the time," he gritted between clenched teeth. Not to mention he loved her. Nothing would make him walk away from her.

"I imagine this killer thought this would get you to step back."

Stromberg crossed his arms in response. He wouldn't be stepping back in any capacity.

Captain Wilson chuckled. "And clearly he doesn't know you at all. Stubborn and obstinate in every way. I tell you to hand in your gun and badge and you act like nothing happened. So, genius, what did you two learn yesterday?"

"That two people who frequent the diner keep a keen eye on Briella. We're currently checking both their alibis thoroughly."

They stared at one another for a long time. Captain Wilson finally broke contact and reached for the top drawer on his desk. He produced Stromberg's gun and badge and set it on the desk closer to his side.

"Don't mess this up. I don't want to hear another peep about you from anyone."

"IA cleared me?"

That fast too? He couldn't hide his shock.

"Some things don't need to go up the chain. Do you think I want this killer to continuously get his way? Because nobody messes with my detectives. I won't be playing his game. So take your badge and gun before I change my mind."

He didn't need to be told twice. Stromberg stood up, clipped his badge back on his belt, and holstered his weapon.

He turned around to leave.

"And Stromberg?"

He looked at the captain.

"If you don't get this guy soon, I can't say how long your secret will stay a secret. If you don't have any intentions of leaving her alone, then you best do your job faster of finding him."

He nodded and walked out. A fire was lit under his ass. Of course he'd be doing his damndest to find this killer. The asshole thought he could threaten Briella, mess with his livelihood, and he wouldn't do a damn thing in return? Wrong! When he found this bastard, there would be hell to pay.

One o'clock rolled around and the meeting with Bryan and his lawyer was something he could sit in on without repercussions anymore.

"Have you ever had a sexual relationship with Dawn?"

Stromberg tried to keep the smirk off his face when Tate

asked the question. He was getting right down to the nitty-gritty of the matter.

"Absolutely not!" Bryan spouted. "Dawn was one of my best friends. She was like a sister to me."

"And Briella?" Stromberg asked as if he wasn't dating her himself.

"I think you'd know if I slept with Briella. She would've told you, seeing as you're sleeping with her now," Bryan shot back.

His lawyer, a douche by the name of Stan Lenicky, turned his stern face in his direction. "Is that true, detective? Are you sleeping with a witness in this case? With the victim's sister?"

Well, shit.

How did Bryan know that? Was he the anonymous sender of the letter? Did that make him the killer?

"I don't see how that's relevant here," he replied, trying to play it off as if it didn't matter. But, oh, it mattered. His captain would have his ass for messing this case up. He could've already handed his ass to the higher-ups but chose not to.

"This interview is over." Stan stood up, gesturing for Bryan to do the same. "I will be filing a grievance against the department for harassment."

They walked out with neither him nor Tate arguing. Bryan even slammed the door on his way out for added effect. It worked. It made him jump in his seat a little.

"I feel like blaming you for that." Stromberg crossed his arms but didn't look at Tate.

"How in the hell is that my fault? I'm not sleeping with a witness."

He snapped his gaze at Tate and glared. "Asshole."

"Jackass."

Stromberg dropped his head, shaking it. "I am a jackass. I just messed up this whole damn case. And if he's our guy, we let him walk out. The captain looked the other way, and now this is happening! He won't be able to look away again."

Tate gripped his shoulder and squeezed, offering comfort—condolences? "A minor setback. Nothing else. If you recall, I did urge you to make a move. So I guess I apologize. It is my fault."

That had him laughing, looking up at him. "Gosh, have you ever apologized to me so much before? Isn't that like three times now?"

"Yeah, well, don't keep expecting it."

Stromberg shoved back his chair, stood up, and blew out a heavy breath. "I guess I should go speak to the captain. Again. I don't want the shit to hit the fan and he take any flack for it. But no matter what happens, I promised Briella I'd find her sister's killer."

Tate stood as well. "Hey, I wanted to kill my sister's killer and things like rules and procedures didn't stop me. Why let it stop you?"

A mangled laugh escaped. "You're a horrible influence. I'm not listening to you."

"We're alike more than you care to admit!" Tate hollered at his back.

He was right.

Nothing and no one would stop him from breaking a promise to Briella.

16

She glanced at her phone, cursing under her breath when it still showed a blank screen. Wyatt hadn't texted all day. She'd sent a few, one with even a big I love you with multiple exclamation points, and nothing. He'd said he was going to have a busy day; she just didn't realize to the point he'd ignore her. Especially since he was suspended. How busy could he be?

The bell above the door jangled, and she frowned. It didn't disappear, even when Detective Rider stopped at the counter with a friendly smile.

"Hey. I'm here to pick you up and bring you home tonight."

Her eyes darted to her phone. Yep. Still a blank screen, no new messages popped up. Then she looked back at him.

"Wyatt didn't tell me that."

He would've told her that.

Rider shrugged, wincing. "He asked me to bring you home. I don't know what to say. You can call him."

She hated to bother him if he was truly busy. But she also couldn't be too trusting. Maybe Rider was the killer.

Her eyes darted to his once again. That damn friendly smile was still plastered on his lips. Relaxed posture. Kind eyes.

What was she thinking? She knew Rider! She'd met him a few times, even went out for drinks one time with a whole bunch of Wyatt's co-workers/friends. Rider had been there as well.

Why suggest she call Wyatt if he was out to harm her? Wyatt would say no I didn't tell him to pick you up and then Rider would do what? Grab her in the middle of the diner with too many witnesses?

"No, if you say he did, I believe you. He must be really busy," she said, sliding her phone into her purse.

Which, again, was odd since he was suspended. Unless...

He'd been arrested or something crazy for being in a relationship with her.

"You have no idea," Rider muttered but didn't elaborate any further.

Oh, no. If he'd gotten into even more trouble because of her...well, he wouldn't like it, but she'd leave him. She'd never let him spend a day in jail because of her. Could one even be arrested for having a relationship with a witness?

She followed him outside where he had miraculously found a spot in front of the diner.

"I won't leave until Wyatt gets home."

She nodded, buckling her seatbelt. "Do you mind bringing me to my apartment? We had planned to pack up some more."

"Yeah, sure."

Though he didn't sound too enthused to help her pack. She wouldn't force him to. He was more than welcome to sit on the couch while she worked, but there was no way she could go to Wyatt's and wait for him. Not without keeping herself busy somehow.

The ride was silent, not filled with tension, but it held an awkwardness she wasn't sure how to decipher.

She sent a text to Wyatt, letting him know Rider was taking her to her apartment instead of his. That would be just as good as calling him to confirm Rider wasn't the bad guy in this situation. Except he didn't respond. Would he even answer if she called?

Her bottom lip ached as she bit hard into it, pondering her dilemma. Before she knew it, Rider was pulling up to her apartment.

"Wait." She had her hand on the handle of the door to shove it open if he said the wrong thing. She was prepared to run for her life. "I didn't give you my address."

He cocked a brow. "Briella, I'm not here to hurt you. Stromberg asked me to take you home and that's what I'm doing. I hate to inform you, but you are the sister of a murder victim. You are involved in these murders because the killer keeps bringing you into the mix. I'm pretty sure half the force knows where you live. When it's one of our own—you are one of us because you're dating Stromberg— then we watch out for each other."

"Did something happen to Wyatt?"

Rider exhaled heavily through his nose. "Well, he's not having a pleasant day. Everything I just said about you being involved in the case, it means Stromberg shouldn't be involved with *you*."

A conflict of interest. Yes, she knew that already. He'd told her all about it.

But they'd been dating for more than a month. The whole department knew about them. Why had it taken his captain a month to do something about it now? What had changed? Why the big deal now? Of course, it didn't help Wyatt didn't know how to stay out of trouble. The moment he'd had his badge taken away, he should've stepped back.

"Can you tell me what happened today?"

Rider shook his head. "You can chat with Stromberg later about it. I don't want to get involved."

She rolled her eyes and shoved open her door. "A little late for that. You brought me home."

Then she stalked to the front door, not bothering to wait for him. He rushed to meet up with her, not falling out of step with her once. She had even been tempted to slam the door in his face, but he was smart enough to read her mind.

Why was she even mad at him? It wasn't his fault Wyatt got into trouble at work. Anything he said, she'd make Wyatt repeat in his own words, so yeah, he made a good point. It would be better to chat with Wyatt about it.

"I'll be in my room packing things up." Then she walked out of the living room without waiting for a reply. She might get why he didn't want to tell her anything, but she was still pissed about it all. She didn't want to say anything else that she'd end up regretting.

She came out a few times to grab something she needed. A box. More newspaper. Each time, Rider looked up from the couch where he sat fiddling with his phone but didn't say anything. She didn't either. She caught him frowning a few times, and sometimes his hand even shook as he held the phone. Like he was filled with rage and wanted to hurl the device against the wall.

Because of Wyatt?

Because of something else?

She knew he wouldn't tell her, so she chose not to ask.

She went back to her room and continued packing her life up.

HE SLID the key into the lock, twisting it slowly. If one did something with extreme patience, it always rewarded the recipient. They thought they could keep him out. Changing her locks wouldn't stop him from his end goal. Little did they know he had a key to the landlord's apartment as well. That idiot didn't change his locks, so it was simply a matter of entering his place, finding her new key, and making a copy. Things couldn't get much easier than that.

He opened the door inch by inch, not wanting to make a sound. He knew she wasn't alone. Not with Detective Stromberg, but still another detective. Brazen and somewhat foolish of him? Most definitely. But he didn't let things like a minor obstacle stop him from what he wanted. Not anymore. He was done waiting. She would be his.

Honestly, they were getting closer to him than he liked. It was now or never. He would have Briella before everything came crumbling down. Once he had her, he'd disappear. Start over. Meet new people and find someone else to love.

The tiny foyer was empty. He shut the door without making a sound. The TV wasn't on. Not much noise to be heard at all.

Odd.

He knew they were moving in together. That she wanted to pack her things up. He figured with Stromberg held up at the precinct she'd want to keep busy. Keep her mind off other things. She'd insist she come here. Yet, he didn't hear anything.

His footsteps made no sound as he inched closer to the living room. A wicked smile grew as he saw the head of the detective who had taken her home. He had no idea which one. It didn't matter.

They would die.

He slid the knife out of the sheath he wore, creeping closer to the couch. Not even a tiny breath released as he took position right behind him. One slash across the throat and even Briella wouldn't know he was here until he was on her.

As he swung the knife to do its bidding, the man twisted at the same time. Instead of cutting his throat in one swift motion, it hit the man's shoulder. He shoved deep, not deterred by the miss.

The man groaned, blood already oozing out. His hand went to his waist to grab his gun, but he was faster than the injured man. He pulled the knife out and shoved it into his body again, this time in the chest.

He snaked his hand down to the man's gun and snuck it behind his back. Then retrieved his knife from his chest and shoved him. He toppled over with ease.

Yep.

This was going to be super easy. No need to even slit his throat.

BRI FROZE IN HER TASK, her jewelry box clutched in her hand.

What was that?

She swore she heard a noise, as if Rider had said something. Which was odd because the man hadn't made a sound all evening. He sat on her couch quiet as a mouse, glaring at his phone. Her phone was in the kitchen where she'd left it after retrieving the last stack of newspaper.

What an idiot! She should have her phone on her at all times, even if she was being protected by a detective.

Her door was open, so she strained her ear to listen. Yet, she couldn't hear anything odd.

Hmm. Maybe she misheard whatever she heard.

But it wouldn't hurt to go out there and make sure.

She rounded her bed where she stood near her dresser and made it halfway to the door when she realized she still held her jewelry box. Dawn had given it to her for her sixteenth birthday. While she didn't wear a whole lot of jewelry, she treasured the few pieces she had because the box itself was something she coveted.

She dashed to the wall at the last second when she swore she heard a light tap, as if someone were walking down the hallway.

Holding her breath, the jewelry box clutched to her chest, she waited. For what? She wasn't sure. All she knew was Rider hadn't moved from his spot once. He'd been glued to his phone, something obviously bothering him. They had come to an understanding. She'd do her thing and not bother him with more questions about Wyatt. And he'd do his thing and not bother her while she sorted her things—and troubled mind.

She saw his foot enter before his face. But she wasn't waiting around to find out who it was. The box felt heavy in her hands, though it was actually light, as she swung it toward the doorframe. The person grunted and staggered back. The box cracked and splintered as it hit his face.

Fighting was not her forte. She didn't even work out at the gym. Defending herself wasn't something she felt comfortable with, but she wasn't about to let him hurt her without a fight.

She rushed forward, shoving him against the hallway

wall, eliciting another grunt from him, surprised by her attack. She didn't wait around to see what else he'd do; she made a mad dash for the living room.

Rider! Why wasn't he helping her?

A scream tore out of her throat when his hard body toppled into her and slammed her to the ground. They wrestled on the floor, and she knew in the pit of her stomach she might die tonight. His strength scared her. With little effort, though she fought hard, he had her turned around so she could see his face.

Heavy breathing filled the space as horror filled her veins.

"Why, Bryan? Why would you do this?"

The bloody knife he held in one hand told her why Rider hadn't come to her rescue. A few drops even plopped onto her cheek. She didn't even flinch at the touch. She was too scared to do anything but stare in terror at what was about to happen.

He'd rape her, then kill her. Just as he had done to Dawn. To those two other women.

"You can at least tell me why before you torture me too!"

His slimy grin twisted her insides with disgust. "I loved Dawn, you know. So much. She never saw me as more than a friend." An ounce of remorse touched his eyes. "I didn't mean to hurt her. I didn't. I don't know what happened that night." Then the evil returned as he gazed hard at her. He traced the bloody knife down her chest, smirking. "But I do know what's going to happen tonight. You'll be mine as was Dawn."

He had lost his mind. Truly and utterly lost his mind. There would be no pleading or begging or talking her way out of this. If she didn't do something—and quick—he'd violate her in the most horrifying manner and then kill her. The worst part wouldn't even be that she had died.

It'd be Wyatt finding her and knowing he would never be able to live with himself for what had happened. For what he'd believe he *let* happen.

"You can be a good girl and enjoy what is about to happen between us"—he twirled the knife in his hand as he sneered—"or you can fight me and make it hurt more than it should. It's your choice."

She swallowed hard, thinking about her options. There weren't many. She would never be able to fight him off. He was right. It would hurt more.

When she didn't move or say anything, his hand reached for her pants, unbuttoning it. The zipper slid down easily too. His pleased smile had her swallowing the bile that had risen up her throat. He was enjoying her torment.

Then his hand went for his pants, unbuttoning and unzipping it. He pulled out his dick and stroked it, his eyes dilating with pleasure.

"You're being such a good girl laying so still. More so than the other ones. They fought so hard."

She swallowed bile back down her throat.

His hand increased in his pleasure. "Move your pants down."

She couldn't. She wouldn't!

The knife scratched her throat when he whipped it to her so fast.

"Don't change your mind now. Dawn fought me. That's part of the reason I stabbed her. I was so angry she fought what could be so magical between us. I don't want to hurt you, Briella. I won't. I love you as much as I loved her." Though the way the knife dug into her throat, she doubted that. "Now do as I say. Pull your pants down."

She let out a shaky breath, then moved her hands to her waist. The knife disappeared from her throat and to his side. His other hand continued to stroke his dick as he watched her shimmy her pants down, albeit awkwardly. It wasn't easy trying to get them off when his heavy weight pressed her to the floor.

But as she wiggled her pants inch by inch, her way out of this dire situation surfaced. The blade of the knife she had tucked behind her pants scraped against her skin.

That's right. She had armed herself for this very moment. How had she forgotten it was behind her?

Bryan was so into pleasuring himself, so proud of himself for her acquiesce, it's as if he trusted her to remain still while he violated her. He closed his eyes.

She took the opportunity to slide her hand from her waist to behind her back and grab the handle of the knife.

His eyes popped open as if he saw her do it.

Pain ricocheted across her body as she sliced herself pulling the knife out from behind her back. He lifted his own knife. But she was faster in her attack.

She swung up and stabbed him right through the neck. Blood spurted, spraying her face. His body jerked. She froze. As if her hand were glued to the handle.

Their eyes met. Triumph and revenge glared out of her eyes. Shock and regret blazed out of his.

Then his body went limp and fell right on top of her. It knocked the sense into her. She screamed, shoving at him until she managed to roll him off.

Her hands were sticky with blood, but it didn't prevent her from pulling her jeans back up. Though the trembles touching her fingers made it impossible to zip and button them.

It took forever for her to get to her feet, the trembles

increasing with strength. She needed her phone. She had to call Wyatt. If he even answered. No problem. She'd call the police. Anybody would work at this point.

When she entered the living room, she saw Rider slumped over on the couch, blood covering his entire chest.

"Oh, no." Her hand went to her mouth as she shuffled to his side a lot faster than she'd risen to her feet. "Oh, shit."

A low, barely audible moan fell from his lips.

"Oh, yes!" she cried, moving him so she could see his chest better. It appeared he'd been stabbed twice. Once in the shoulder and one that looked dangerously close to his heart. She grabbed the sunflower blanket she used when bingeing her favorite shows and shoved it against the wound near his heart. Another, more audible, moan escaped.

"Stay with me, Rider! Do you hear me! No one but that asshole himself is dying tonight."

She darted her gaze around until she saw Rider's phone that had fallen to the floor. It was locked. She had no idea what his passcode could be, and he was incapable of telling her. She feared he was close to dying more than anything else.

If she let off any kind of pressure from his chest, she knew he wouldn't make it. He still might not.

But that was the nice thing about phones these days. They had emergency features. No need to unlock the phone to call 9-1-1.

So that's what she did.

17

HE'D BEEN STUCK in a conference room all day. Talking to his captain. Talking to Internal Affairs. After telling his captain about the threat from the lawyer, an hour later it wasn't a threat anymore. At least they hadn't shoved him into an interrogation room like he was a suspect. It didn't make the day go by any better. They rarely even let him out to use the bathroom. His phone hadn't been allowed in the room either. He figured he should at least be grateful that they allowed him to relay a message to Rider and asked him to pick up Briella. She wasn't safe by herself.

Tate was busy working the case and trying to nail Bryan's ass with anything. Especially since the bastard had ratted him out about his relationship with Briella. How had he known about it?

The three murder cases were being torn apart and picked through as if he'd done something to mess it up on purpose. He couldn't help he fell in love. But it hadn't distracted him from the ultimate goal: finding the killer.

Not even Tate's vocal—and rather rude—words had

helped his case. He was in hot water, and losing his job would be on the horizon soon.

It wouldn't stop him from protecting Briella and finding the killer. Tate had been right about that. Take his job. Take his gun and badge. But they wouldn't take his fight to keep her safe.

It was nearing seven o'clock. The two detectives from IA had left the room ten minutes ago, and he'd sat alone for the entire time. All it did was make him swirl with worry about Briella. How was she doing? Was Rider handling her okay? He knew the guy was going through his own issues at the moment. What they were, he wasn't exactly sure, but he'd seen the tension he'd been wearing the last week or so. But when someone didn't want to talk about something, Stromberg was the last person to make them do so. He didn't talk about his personal life much either.

The door burst open with a harried Tate.

"Call just came in for Briella's apartment."

Stromberg shoved his chair back so hard he nearly toppled the large table. He followed Tate out of the room, not caring about the consequences. They could lock him up for leaving.

Tate drove, speeding like a madman. He didn't even argue to take the wheel. He would've crashed the car with the way the anxiety was coursing through his veins.

The killer had made a move.

The fact a call came in showed good signs, but how good?

They made it there in record time, but still not fast enough. He ran the two flights of stairs instead of waiting for the elevator. Tate was hot on his heels. He only slammed on the brakes in the living room when the pool of blood on the couch stalled his movements. So much blood it tore his heart apart.

Briella.

His sweet, beautiful Briella.

"Yo, it's not her blood. Rider's fighting for his life right now," Thompson said in a quiet, subdued voice.

Stromberg tore his gaze away from the bloodied couch and to him. "Briella? Where is she?"

"She's fine. She wasn't here when I got here—five minutes ago—but I'm told she's fine."

Well, Stromberg wouldn't believe that until he saw it with his own eyes.

Thompson pointed to the hallway. "You're instincts, as usual, were right." He grinned like the devil. "And you have a helluva girlfriend. She took him down like the fighter she is."

Tate took the lead and Stromberg followed. The crime scene crew was already there and doing their job. How did they get here so fast? Or had they been notified too late?

Lying faceup with a knife still stuck in his throat was Bryan. The bastard had been the killer. His pants were halfway down and his dick lying limp but visible.

That rotten, dirty—

Tate grabbed ahold of his shoulder as if he sensed Stromberg was about to lose his shit. "Let's go to the hospital."

He didn't argue. The anger and disgust filling him up overrode any other senses. He was quiet the entire ride. Tate chose to remain silent as well.

Tate did most of the talking when they entered the hospital. He inquired about Rider, and Stromberg couldn't even be mad about it. He was their friend, their fellow officer. Of course he wanted Rider to pull through. If not for him asking Rider to pick up Briella, he wouldn't be fighting for his life right now.

The nurse informed them he was in surgery and it was too soon to tell.

Then Tate asked about Briella. A smile warmed her tired features and she gestured for them to follow her. A curtain pulled to the side by the same nurse revealed Briella sitting up and a doctor stitching her side.

"Briella, baby!" He rushed to her side, but he knew he couldn't pull her into his arms and distract the doctor.

The man did pop up his head but then went back to his task.

She wrapped her hand around his and closed her eyes. "I've been so worried about you."

"Why?" He brushed her cheek, prompting her to open her eyes. "You're the one who was nearly killed."

"You didn't text all day. You didn't answer any of the texts I sent. Rider said it was a horrible day for you but wouldn't tell me why."

He brought his other hand up, cupping both cheeks. "It doesn't matter anymore."

And it didn't. It shouldn't anyway. Cases closed. Killer dead. No need to go to trial and convict.

Of course that didn't mean his job wasn't still on the line. IA could fire him for his behavior, for getting involved with a witness.

He leaned closer, pressing his forehead to hers, then whispered, "Did he...did he try...his pants were down."

God, he couldn't even get the full question out. Why should he expect her to tell him all the sordid details?

"He tried." Her hand went to his side and gripped it, her nails dragging across his skin. "It was his mistake. Because while he thought I was being the docile victim, he let his enjoyment distract him. I had my knife to help me."

He pulled away a fraction, brimming from ear to ear. "I'm glad you killed that bastard."

Her lips wobbled. "He killed Dawn."

"I know, baby. I know." His forehead rested against hers again.

All he wanted to do was pull her hard into his embrace. Finally, a few short minutes later, the doctor informed him he could. He didn't hesitate. He moved Briella over a bit, then picked her up and planted her in his lap, crushing her to his chest. The sobs tore out of her.

Tate pulled the curtain closed, leaving the two of them alone. Not that it stopped from everyone hearing her crying on the other side of the curtain, but at least they couldn't see her while she did so.

He held her, trying to infuse as much of the strength he had left into her. She'd need it for the coming days. The police—he wouldn't be able to do it—would need her official statement of events. Even after she did all that, she would have to live with the fact she killed a man.

The same man who had murdered her sister and two other women, but still. She had killed a man.

And he'd be right by her side through it all.

"So, like, did Stromy say anything about his job yet?" Abby asked as she bit into a carrot and then chomped away like it wasn't annoying.

She did chew with her mouth closed, but the chomping was still loud. Though, the last few days, everything, every little sound had been amplified. Bri couldn't be sure why. If she hadn't heard the soft footsteps, things could've gone a completely different way. So she wouldn't complain too much about her intensified hearing.

"Yo!" Abby said, snapping her fingers.

Bri blinked, then looked up from the broccoli she had been cutting into smaller pieces. "Ummm...they slapped him on the wrist, whatever that means," she rolled her eyes at his version of the story, "and he can go back to work next week." They'd suspended him for the week, so perhaps that's what he meant by a slap on the wrist. As far as she knew, they hadn't penalized him in any other way. She didn't think Wyatt would keep that information from her. At least, she hoped he wouldn't. Being honest in all aspects of their lives was important. She knew he knew that.

She couldn't be bothered by the suspension either. He was home with her. Right now, that's what she needed. She hadn't been back to her apartment since it all happened two days ago. She didn't think she'd ever be able to walk back in there. The memories. The things that happened. It was all too much.

Wyatt understood that, which was why he was there with Tate packing up the rest of her belongings while she and Abby prepared food for when they got back. She might've gone overboard shopping, but she had to occupy her time with something. Abby understood that. So had Wyatt.

"That's good. I know he loves his job as much as Tate does. I mean, he didn't do anything wrong, per se."

Yeah, only slept with her and could've ruined the entire case by getting involved with a witness. She got it. She knew why they took him in for questioning.

"Are you okay?"

She looked up from the broccoli, stared at the concern in

Abby's eyes, and then followed her gaze as it led back to the knife wobbling in her hand. She set it down and took a few staggering steps backward.

"If I hadn't had that knife, he would've raped me, I would've let him, and then he would've killed me."

"This is something only Tate and Stromy know. Like nobody else. My brother did, but he's dead and he doesn't count."

She wrapped her arms around herself as Abby continued.

"I was a hot mess when Tate found out my brother killed his sister. He wanted to kill him, no matter the consequences. I wanted to stop him and make him do the right thing. He wouldn't listen. I thought it would be wise to inform his captain about what he was doing. I changed my mind at the last second and I thought that was that. Until he showed up at my house and things took a crazy turn. The official report says my brother killed Captain Monroe because he was done following his orders."

Abby paused, and Bri waited with bated breath. She knew most of the story. Not all the dirty details, but Wyatt had given her a brief breakdown, considering they spent a lot of time with Tate and Abby. He didn't want there to be any secrets between them. So most of what Abby told her she already knew.

Abby released a breath. "He tried to attack me, and I fought back. He fell and hit his head on the edge of the fireplace. I've never seen so much blood before. I panicked and I tried to clean it up. I rolled him up in a tarp and shoved him under my patio in the backyard."

Bri's eyes widened in shock.

"So I know how it feels to kill someone. I get what you're going through."

"Oh, my gosh, Abby. And they think your brother did it?"

"He did horrible things. Killed too many people and some who didn't deserve it. But my brother loved me, and he made sure I wouldn't get in trouble for it. He had his way of showing the world he could be good despite all the bad."

Abby popped another carrot in her mouth, chewing slower this time. "I'm not sad Captain Monroe is dead. He was a horrible man. He abused his position and treated others as if they didn't matter. I struggle some nights at what I did, but mostly, I'm not sorry."

Bri drew her gaze to the floor, swirling her foot in a circle. "I'm not sorry about Bryan either." Then her gaze became level again. "Does that make us bad people thinking that way?"

Abby shrugged nonchalantly. "Why should it? We were defending ourselves. What were we supposed to do? Let it happen?" She slammed her hand on the counter, surprising Bri and making her flinch. "I'm not about to let anyone walk all over me, especially a disgusting degrading man like Captain Monroe."

"Bryan was delusional. He lost it when my sister didn't reciprocate his feelings. Then his twisted mind turned it on to me. He was sick." She nodded as if Abby had said something she agreed with, even though she stood quietly waiting for her to finish. "I'd do it again if I had to. Part of me relishes the idea I got the right kind of justice for Dawn. I'm glad he's dead and not sitting in a prison cell."

"You did the world a favor." Abby picked up her wineglass instead of another carrot and held it out to her. "To protecting ourselves. To not letting the assholes win. And to falling in love with the most stubborn, obstinate men on the planet. You know Stromy isn't going to make things easy on you any more than Tate makes things easy on me."

Bri picked up her glass and clinked it with hers. "That's what keeps things interesting and alive between us."

Abby smiled as she took a sip. "Oh, yes, the makeup sex, sometimes even angry sex is so good I find ways to get him riled up."

Bri giggled, then took an even bigger sip. More like a gulp. "I might have to try that sometime."

She felt lighter and like a huge weight had lifted off her shoulders after they chatted. To know they shared in something so horrifying together, she couldn't even find the right words for it.

They spent a wonderful day together, sipping on wine and eating food. Sometimes, the fresh fruit and vegetables they cut up, and sometimes junk food that hit the craving she couldn't hit otherwise.

When Wyatt returned with Tate, they both saw how tired the men were, and Abby shuffled her and Tate out the door with minimal fuss. Wyatt took a shower, and she was waiting in bed when he got out with a towel wrapped around his waist.

She held out her arms for him to cuddle with her. He obliged but, before he could get dressed and climb in bed, she stopped him with a wag of her finger.

"Lose the towel and don't put on any clothes."

He smiled, letting it drop to the floor, then slid into bed, pulling her into his arms. She'd been resting under the covers, so he didn't realize she was naked too until he had her in his embrace.

He brushed a tender hand across her head and down her back. "We got it all packed and to the donation center.

I'll have a cleaning crew there tomorrow, and it'll be ready for the landlord to do as he wishes."

After much debate, and not wanting to worry about what should go where, she told Wyatt to get rid of it all. The things she wanted she had already packed and brought to his place. They were piled in his living room waiting for her to do something with it all. Everything else, it didn't matter.

"Thank you."

"Baby, I'll always take care of you. You never have to thank me for that."

She wiggled in his arms until she had her head resting on his chest and contentment finally found a place in her soul. No one was out there to hurt her anymore. Her life was on a better track. Best of all, she had Wyatt in her arms.

"How's Rider doing?" She'd been too afraid to call the hospital and inquire again. The news hadn't been good the day before.

"He lost a lot of blood. He's still in the ICU. But they're hopeful."

She felt Wyatt shiver, and not from any cold air caressing his skin. "It's not your fault, you know."

"Yeah, well, it shouldn't have been him."

She hugged him tighter. "And I wouldn't have wanted it to be you."

They lay in silence, not the uncomfortable kind either. It felt nice to hold him and settle into a quiet peace. For so long—the past year—her life had been nothing but chaos and turmoil. It felt odd, yet refreshing to be able to not let anything plague her mind.

She nearly dozed off when Wyatt's low, rumbled tone alerted her senses.

"Let me know when you're ready for anything...more. I

know what he did wasn't all the way, but it was still very violating. I would never rush you."

She lifted her head and placed a hand on his bearded cheek, rubbing it and loving the sweet way his eyes blazed with desire.

"And for that, I love you even more. I'm not sure when I'll be ready."

He bent his head, kissing her forehead with such tenderness she wanted to cry for some reason. "And I'll wait patiently, baby."

He was a man of his word. It took her three weeks before she felt ready to do anything more than just lie in his arms with nothing between them but love.

EPILOGUE

Four months later

"You know, you still don't have to bring me to work every day and pick me up, right?" she said with her lips grazing his as if he wouldn't stop kissing her if she didn't keep it light.

"But I like doing it." His tongue darted in, sweeping a beautiful moan out of her. "And it helps to stop me from working too much and come rushing to you."

Because, besides Briella, work consumed his life. He took pride in closing cases and finding closure for victims. Sure, he had a red mark against him, written in his file, that he'd crossed a line when he slept with Briella *and* worked her sister's murder. But whatever. That hadn't impeded his job or his focus on the case. If anything, it had ramped it up.

He found the killer. They had brought Bryan in for questioning. His lawyer had thwarted their efforts, but in the end, because Bryan had been too greedy in his lust, he'd wrapped the case up himself. The bastard deserved everything that happened to him.

"Remember, I made a reservation at the bakery for six. But I want to go home and take a shower and look respectable. So, you have to be here at four thirty, not five o'clock."

"I got it. I won't be late."

He'd proposed two months ago because he knew what he wanted: Briella in his life until the day he died. Thankfully, she had felt the same way, saying yes. Tate and Abby had gotten married last month at the courthouse, wanting little fanfare. Stromberg liked to joke with him that *he* was the one who put the bug in his ear to even talk to Abby about marriage. The asshole still liked to deny it to this day.

Tate and Abby didn't have family. They had very few friends. Stromberg was about the only guy in the precinct who could stand Tate for more than an hour. Hell, he loved the guy like he was his brother. He'd call him his best friend if anyone asked. So for them to throw a lavish wedding didn't make sense. Not a lot of people would be invited anyway.

For him, it was a different matter. Of course, he had told Briella all about his mom and dad, mentioning he didn't have contact with his mother any longer. But he also had a brother and a sister. Sure, he didn't see them very often, but they were his family. They had been a lot younger when their father died. It hadn't messed them up as much as him. They even still spoke to their mother.

On his mother's side, he had a few aunts and uncles he spoke to as well. They had been happy to hear the news of their upcoming nuptials. It gave them an excuse to get together, since they rarely did. While Briella didn't have any family to attend, she had reached out to her friends she'd lost contact with. Amends were made, and her life was starting to look like it had before her sister had been killed.

So they had to plan an actual wedding, if only to make his family and her friends happy. Her three girlfriends had jumped at the chance to be bridesmaids before she could even ask them. He'd be okay doing what Tate and Abby had done, but he wouldn't take this moment away from Briella. Because from the moment he asked for her hand in marriage, she had jumped all in.

In another five months, they'd be wed.

She grabbed him by the lapels of his wool coat, squinted her eyes as if laser beaming the horrid things she'd do to him if he were late, then smacked another soul-crushing kiss to his lips.

"I can't wait to taste test all the flavors tonight."

And neither could he just to see the happiness brimming from her eyes.

After one more kiss because he couldn't resist, he left and headed for the precinct. Tate was already at his desk, combing through the latest case that had landed on their desk late yesterday afternoon. A child's death, no less. They were the worst, and no detective liked to deal with them.

He took his seat and picked up the coffee cup Tate had grabbed for him from the local cafe around the corner. "Thanks." He winced when he realized it had creamer or some shit in it. He twisted the cup and gave Tate a stony look. "This isn't even for me."

Tate looked up from his papers and blinked as if he hadn't even realized Stromberg had sat down. "What?" Then he looked at the cup and shrugged. "I've had a lot on my mind." He tapped the paper in front of him hard, not that Stromberg could see what it was. "I think it was the father who did it. We need to speak to him again. Now."

Tate stood up, and Stromberg didn't argue. Except he needed to do one thing.

"I want my coffee first."

Then he walked away before Tate could argue, not that it would make a difference. He stopped in front of Rider's desk, his heart beating rapidly. It always did when he spoke to him since everything happened.

Rider looked up, expressionless. He'd miraculously recovered from being stabbed twice, one way too close to his heart. But since being released from the hospital, he wasn't the man Stromberg had come to know. Whoever the person sitting in the chair in front of him was, it wasn't Rider. It wasn't his old friend.

"I, um, think our coffees got mixed up."

He twisted his cup so Rider could see his name written on the cup he held. Though it said Ryder instead of the way he actually spelled it. Most of the baristas at the cafe knew them, and whenever one of them went in to order, they asked for the usual and nobody needed to be told what that was. He and Tate liked their coffee solid black, Rider liked his with vanilla flavoring added, and Vance and Roco liked a touch of sugar in theirs.

Rider waved a hand at the cup sitting on the corner of his desk. Probably in the same spot Tate had delivered it. He set the cup down and nodded with a smile as he picked up the other one.

"Thanks."

Rider went back to the paperwork in front of him without uttering one word.

"We're having people over this weekend for the game. You'll be there." Stromberg made it a point to say it more as a statement than a question. He wanted whatever this awkward shit between them was to disappear. He wanted to go back to the days when Rider clapped him jovially on the back for no reason other than to say hi.

"Na, can't this weekend." Then he went back to his papers and dismissed Stromberg as if they hadn't ever been good friends.

Well, one no—in a long line of nos—wouldn't stop him from breaking the shell Rider had erected around himself.

He'd keep at it.

Because that's what he did when a problem loomed before him. Whether it be a frustrating, puzzling case, or a friend who was sorely in need of saving.

Unfortunately, Rider needed saving from himself.

He left with Tate, revealing his worries about Rider. With one simple nod, he knew he had Tate in his corner. Even though he didn't get along with everyone, Tate was trying harder to be more mellow and not so rigid.

When he relayed it to Briella tonight, he knew she'd be in one hundred percent.

Honestly, the only time he saw even a hint of a smile from Rider was when Briella was in his presence.

If anyone could get through to him, it'd be her.

For Tate & Abby's story
Dark Consequences
A Consequences Novel, #1

Every choice has a consequence...

Detective Tate Powell lives for one thing: revenge against the man who killed his sister. But when he discovers that man is none other than his girlfriend Abby's brother, his world shatters.

Torn between loyalty to her troubled brother and her feelings for Tate, Abby faces an impossible choice. She must betray the man she loves to protect her family. Even if it means turning against Tate forever.

As Tate's thirst for vengeance spirals out of control, he risks losing Abby and damning his own soul. Will he choose retribution or redemption before he loses Abby forever?

With gut-wrenching twists and taut suspense, this gripping thriller will leave romantic suspense fans on the edge of their seats. Find out in the explosive first book of the Consequences series!

One decision can have fatal consequences...

Detective Rider's life is spiraling. After nearly dying in the line of duty, now he's saddled with two babysitters as partners and an attitude problem his captain won't let slide. Just when he thinks his luck can't get any worse, he's thrown a case involving a woman who shattered his heart years ago—and the best friend he was forced to leave behind.

Junelle Swanson thought she'd moved on after Rider walked away. Until her dog is brutally killed and threatening letters start arriving, giving her no choice but to trust the man who broke her heart. She just wishes her brother Jason, who welcomes his former best friend back with open arms, wouldn't ask uncomfortable questions about the past that Rider isn't ready to answer.

As the investigation intensifies, clues surface, pointing to a sinister threat lurking closer than they imagined. With a killer watching their every move and their past feelings complicating everything, Rider and Junelle must confront both their painful past and a deadly present before they become the next victims.

*Perfect for fans of high-stakes thrillers who crave their love stories with a dangerous edge. One-click **Fatal Consequences** now and discover how far one detective will go to protect the woman he never stopped loving.*

FOR JASON & VICTORIA'S STORY
VICIOUS CONSEQUENCES
A CONSEQUENCES NOVEL, #4

No good deed goes unpunished.

Jason Swanson thought he was done being a victim. After barely surviving an attack that left him jumping at shadows, he refuses to stand by when he witnesses a vicious assault. Except his heroism backfires when he's arrested for the crime. Worse, the lead detective is the same woman who shot him down at his best friend's wedding.

Detective Victoria Johansen is tough as nails when it comes to her job, even if she's awkward around everyone else. When she realizes she arrested the wrong man, she's strong enough to admit her mistake. What she doesn't expect is her growing attraction to Jason—a man who sees past her oddness to the woman beneath.

As their relationship deepens, the real killer emerges from the shadows, turning their investigation into a deadly game of cat and mouse. But they have no idea how close the danger really is. Or that the killer has been watching them all along.

*Perfect for readers who crave pulse-pounding romantic suspense with jaw-dropping twists. One-click **Vicious Consequences** now to start this edge-of-your-seat thriller today!*

ABOUT THE AUTHOR

I'm a *USA Today* Bestselling Author that loves to write contemporary romance and romantic suspense novels, although I am partial to romantic suspense. I even dabble in paranormal. Honestly, I love anything that has to do with romance. As long as there's a happy ending, I'm a happy camper. And insta-love...yes, please! I love baseball (Go Twins!) and creating awesome crafts. I graduated with a Bachelor's Degree in Criminal Justice, working in that field for several years before I became a stay-at-home mom. I have a few more amazing stories in the works. If you would like to learn more about me and my books, head to my website by scanning the QR code. Thanks for reading!

Scan me

www.ingramcontent.com/pod-product-compliance
Lightning Source LLC
Chambersburg PA
CBHW030537030726
47495CB00004B/1027